A
BONNET
FOR VIRGINIA

by Evelyn M. Frantz

THE BRETHREN PRESS

ELGIN, ILL.

A BONNET FOR VIRGINIA

Copyright © 1978, by the Brethren Press

Printed in the United States of America

Library of Congress Cataloging in Publication Data:

Frantz, Evelyn M., 1927-
  A Bonnet for Virginia.

[1. Family life—Fiction. 2. Nebraska—Fiction] I. Title.
PZ7.F85925Bo   [Fic]   78-6472

ISBN 0-87178-101-8

Published by the Brethren Press, Elgin, Ill.

Distributed by Two Continents Publishing Group,
30 E. 42 St., New York, N.Y. 10017

CONTENTS

Dedicated to
Virginia and Ira's Children:
Dale
Bernice
Greta
Gladys
Lyle
Duane
with special thanks to Gladys
for her encouragement and help

Chapter 1.
LUNCH HOURS

Virgie curled her toes inside the long, blue-and-white striped stockings her father had knit for her and tried to shrink into the seat of her school desk. All the other girls were watching Queenie Shay. Queenie had long blond curls, which her mother tied in rags every night, and a ring on her fat little hand. She lived in one of the nicest houses in town and her mother had short hair. Virgie knew only two ladies with short hair, and she knew the other women spoke disapprovingly of them.

All the girls watched as Queenie opened the painted metal lunch box her mother's hired girl had brought to school. First Queenie took out a snowy white napkin, shook it out with a grand gesture and smoothed it carefully on her desk. Then she lifted out a package of sandwiches, a piece of chocolate cake, an apple, a wedge of cheese, some kind of pastry. Giving a little giggle, she quickly closed the lid as if she wanted to hide the other things.

Virgie swallowed hard and reached into the lard pail beside her. She already knew it held some cold cornbread and a small piece of meat left from last night's supper. Virgie had packed the lunch herself that morning when she and her sister Pearl were getting ready for school. She looked across the circle and found Pearl watching her. Pearl understands how I feel, Virgie thought. I know I'm supposed to like everyone, but I sure don't like Queenie. Listen to her bragging!

7

"Oh, dear," Queenie was saying. "Helga knows I don't like beef sandwiches. I want ham. I must tell Mother to speak to her again, and Mother'll probably discharge her. You just can't get good help these days!"

Dot Burden choked on her boiled egg and Virgie grinned to herself. Dot's sister was "working out" for a town family, as many of the older girls did. They all knew Mrs. Shay was a hard woman to please and here was Queenie, acting just like her.

Virgie knew as well as anyone that Nebraska hadn't had enough rain for several years, not since 1891 anyway. That was three years ago, and people were getting more discouraged all the time. No rain meant no crops and no crops meant no money. Virgie's father and the other men talked about it whenever they got together. And last year they'd had a Panic. Virgie still didn't really understand what it was, but she knew that banks had closed and there weren't any jobs. People were giving up their farms and homesteads and moving away.

Swallowing the last of the dry cornbread, Virgie replaced the lid on her lard pail and carried it to the cloakroom, trying not to notice the delicious smell of Queenie's chocolate cake. The younger children had eaten their lunch and were already on the playground, the little girls playing tag and the boys shooting marbles.

Virgie was thirsty, but the big boys were hanging around the pump and its tin cup outside, so she lingered in the cloakroom. Her light brown hair was pulled back from her blue eyes and tied with a big bow. Then it fell in one thick braid down her back. The brown plaid dress she wore was faded and too short. Virgie was afraid she looked as awkward as she often felt. She knew there was no money to pay the dressmaker for new clothes when her old ones got too short, but seeing the pretty dresses Queenie wore didn't help her feelings.

In a moment Dot and Pearl also came in to put their lunch pails on the long shelf above the coat rack. Pearl, Virgie's sister, had gray green eyes in a square face and

8

tight little curls on top of her head. Dot had dark hair and sallow skin.

"Isn't that Queenie awful?" Dot whispered. "She thinks she's so smart, putting on all those airs and tossing her head around so grand!"

Virgie was puzzled. "She just lives right here in town. Usually she goes home to eat. Why did she send over for her lunch today?" she asked, watching Pearl puff out her curls.

"Oh, don't you know what she does?" Pearl asked. "When Mr. Mason excuses her to get a drink, she comes out here and peeks into our pails to see what we have. Then she tells little Dolly Jones to stop by her house and tell them to send her lunch over, so she can show off and brag."

"Oh, Pearl, does she really do that?" Virgie gasped. Dot nodded.

"Here's Maggie Peterson. Just ask her," Dot said as Maggie came in. "Maggie, didn't you see Queenie peeking in the lunch pails?"

"I certainly did. And now she's in there just waiting for us to leave, so she can pass around her *candy* to her *special* friends," Maggie sniffed. "I'm not going to stay and watch. She makes me sick! Let's get a drink."

They took turns at the pump handle, while each one got a drink. As the handle squeaked loudly the water gushed out, spilling over the tin cup and making a mud puddle at the base of the pump. The girls stood carefully away from the mud and leaned over with the cup, hoping the water wouldn't splash their clothes.

"What'll we do?" asked Maggie, wiping her mouth with her hand.

"Let's go round back and talk," Dot answered.

Virgie looked at the younger children still playing tag. The November day was unusually cold and running around would help her keep warm. But she was thirteen now and must try to act grown-up. In another year or two she'd be a young lady and she'd better start practicing.

"I wanted to tell you about my sister Sally," Dot continued. "She told me she and Jake Fedders are just about to have an 'understanding'. That means he's not going to walk anyone else to church and she's not going to dance with anyone else at parties."

Virgie looked at Pearl. "I wonder if Katie and George have an understanding?"

"Who's George?" Maggie asked.

"He writes to our sister Katie. He used to take her places when we lived in Kansas," Pearl said. "She must've got a letter just the other day. I saw one on the clock shelf."

"Well, why don't you read it? When my sister gets a letter I always read it. I like to see all that lovey-dovey stuff that boys write to girls," Maggie giggled.

"Oh, that wouldn't be right! You shouldn't touch other people's mail," Virgie gasped.

Dot shrugged. "Who's gonna know? You could read it in a few minutes and then put it right back. Besides, as Maggie says, there's a lot of good stuff in letters from a boy. My cousin snitched one from her sister and we read it and— ooh, la, la." She rolled her eyes and fell onto Maggie's shoulder while they both laughed loudly. Virgie felt foolish. She was relieved to hear Mr. Mason ring the hand bell to start school for the afternoon.

"Come on, Pearl. Let's get at the head of the line. I don't want to stand by the boys," Virgie said. They raced around the building to get in line.

The big boys came sauntering toward the door, pretending they weren't in line. Virgie noticed that Queenie Shay and her friends were at the end of the girls' line, where the boys would be sure to notice them. She shivered, hoping Mr. Mason would not insist on perfect attention.

Inside again, Virgie bent to pull her grammar and her speller from her desk. I wonder what's really in Katie's letter, she thought.

10

Chapter 2.
THE LETTER

When school was out Virgie and Pearl bundled themselves in shawls and mittens and began the walk home. Sometimes they went to the post office or store in the little village of Shrevesville before starting home, but today their father had been in town, so there were no errands. The wind had turned colder and the sky had filled with heavy, gray clouds. Occasionally hard grains of sleet fell, clattering on the hard ground.

"Aren't we lucky the schoolhouse is on the edge of town, so we only have a mile to walk?" asked Pearl, shivering inside her shawl.

"Yes. We live closer than any of the country scholars," Virgie replied.

The strong wind swept across the cold, empty land, which lay in various shades of brown beneath the gray sky. It tore at the girls, almost taking their breath away, as they struggled over the ridge that separated their farm home from the valley where the village lay. Virgie was glad when the ridge began to shelter them slightly. From here she could look down on the farm her father rented.

The small gray farmhouse stood on the side of a hill. On one side of the house the ground broke away abruptly to a deep "draw" or ravine. The farm buildings—the corncrib, the chicken house, some sheds—were also sheltered by the hill. The barn was built into the hillside, with the upper entrance for storing hay and the stable beneath it.

11

Virgie and Pearl walked closer together as they came within sight of their home. The wind was not so strong now, and they could talk more easily. "Pearl, do you think Katie's letter says what Maggie said?" asked Virgie timidly.

Pearl tucked her cold hands under her arms. "I don't know."

"We could read it fast and put it right back, like they said," Virgie suggested.

"Yes, I suppose we could," Pearl replied. "We really shouldn't, but maybe we could find out if they have an 'understanding.' "

They ran the last few steps down the hill, through the lane and burst into the back door. Virgie could never remember anyone using the front door. It opened into the "front" room, which they hardly ever used.

The kitchen was large and cheerful. The big, round table where they ate, wrote, studied and worked was covered with brightly flowered oilcloth. The iron cookstove was big and warm and Katie kept its black surface shining. Small braided rugs, made from their worn-out clothes, lay on the board floor in front of the sagging daybed.

As she warmed her hands at the stove, Virgie stole a glance at the clock shelf above the window. Yes, there was an envelope just peeking out from behind the clock.

Virgie's heart beat faster as she looked at Pearl, who was two years older than Virgie, but only a little taller. Her blue plaid dress, made like Virgie's, was also faded and too short. Pearl was thin and not very strong, but she and Virgie had been special pals ever since they could remember.

Virgie motioned to the clock shelf. "Do you think we can take it now?" she whispered.

"Better wait to see where Katie is," Pearl whispered back. "I think she's coming."

The girls heard a door close upstairs and their sister's steps coming toward the kitchen. Katie had been their "mother" ever since their own mother had died when Virgie was only three. Now she was grown up and Virgie hoped she'd be as pretty as Katie some day. As she entered the

12

room, Virgie looked at her admiringly. Katie had a square face, blue eyes and high forehead. She wore her brown hair piled up on her head and had bangs that she curled with tin curlers.

"Hello, girls," Katie said pleasantly. "It's cold out today, isn't it? Warm up good before you start your evening work. Elizabeth's out helping Father. Virgie, I think we'll need an extra basket of cobs tonight, since the men haven't gotten much wood hauled yet and we're having this cold snap."

"All right. I'll change my clothes right away." Somehow Virgie was glad to leave the room. It was chilly in the room she shared with Pearl, next to Father's room. Besides, she didn't feel quite right in front of Kate. She fumbled with the buttons on her dress, hung it over a chair so it wouldn't be too wrinkled for school the next day, and slipped into the older "everyday" dress she wore at home. Pearl came in and began to change, too.

"I'll go out and gather cobs right now," Virgie whispered. "You can start peeling potatoes and when Katie goes to feed the chickens you come on out to the stable with the letter."

"All right."

Putting on a sweater and fastening a shawl about her, Virgie ran out the door and picked up the cob basket. Dried corn cobs made good fuel, but since it was only November and this year's corn crop had just been gathered, there weren't many cobs lying around the corn crib and barn. Virgie decided to look in the pig pen. Katie couldn't see her as well there, and Virgie got a funny feeling whenever Katie looked at her today.

Virgie had to pry the rough cobs out of the frozen ground, and she wished Pearl would hurry. After awhile she saw Katie going toward the chicken house and her heart beat faster. Soon Pearl would be coming. What was that "lovey-dovey stuff" Maggie was talking about? Why had she and Dot laughed in such a silly way?

Virgie was wondering so hard she didn't hear Pearl coming. She jumped when Pearl said, "Come on, Virgie, quick!"

13

Leaving the cob basket, she and Pearl ran toward the stable. It was warmer in there, out of the wind. They settled down in a pile of hay and Pearl pulled the letter from her pocket.

The fancy writing on the envelope said

"Miss Catherine W. Wine
Shrevesville
Butler County, Nebraska"

Pearl's fingers trembled a little as she took out the folded paper. Virgie, impatient, snatched it from her and together the girls read:

"Dear Katie,

It has been awhile since I have written, so I will say the livery stable business has done tolerably well recently. I have added two more bays to the stable, but will have to sell the roan mare, as she is getting too old. I also got another top buggy, as the other one has never been too good since it broke down last fall.

I was out at your Uncle Sam's last week. They seem well and said to send your family their regards. Your friend Anna Pottenger also wants you to know she is well and will write when she is not so busy with the baby. You know she and Phil have two now and Phil is working very hard in the blacksmith shop he built on their farm.

The railroad that David and Mike helped build has three trains a day now, so we are getting quite civilized out here in western Kansas. Pretty soon we'll be as crowded as you are back there in the East. Ha, ha!

Please give the boys my regards and convey my respects to your father. That is all the news for now, so no more at present.

Yours affectionately,
George McKibbin"

"But—but where is all—all that stuff Maggie was talking about?" Virgie gasped. Pearl reached for the letter.

14

"I don't know. Let's read it again. You pulled the paper so hard, I couldn't see it too well. Maybe I missed it." The girls read the letter again, but it said no more and no less than it had the first time. "Well, it's not there," Pearl said decidedly. "Maggie just didn't know what she was talking about. But goodness, Virgie, wouldn't it be nice to go back to Uncle Sam's again and see our cousins?"

"I wonder if the little sod house on our homestead is still there or if it's fallen down by now," Virgie sighed. "I'm sure the cottonwoods are still growing. Remember how Father planted them when we moved there and how tall they grew before we left? I was so sad to leave Kansas, but now I feel this is home. I love this hill farm." Pearl got to her feet.

"I do too, but we'd better get this letter back in the house and get to work before Katie misses us," she said practically.

"You're right, but those cobs are sure hard to dig out of frozen ground," Virgie sighed.

As Virgie carried the basket of cobs into the house later, a thought struck her. "Say, Pearl," she whispered, "since that letter doesn't have any—any of that stuff in, does that mean Katie and George don't have an 'understanding'?"

"I guess not, Virgie."

As she set the table for supper Virgie had a strange feeling of disappointment. She didn't know if it was her conscience hurting her for reading Katie's letter, or if she was sorry she couldn't go to school and brag about Katie's 'understanding' when Dot and Maggie were talking about their sisters.

At twilight Elizabeth and her father came. Elizabeth was seventeen, four years older than Virgie. She was tall and slim, with dark, windblown hair and skin still burned brown from her summer outdoors. She loved to ride her horse over the prairie at full speed. Virgie sometimes worried that the horse would step in a gopher hole and Lizzie, as they had always called her, would be thrown off.

Virgie ran to her father's arms, knowing she would hear his usual greeting, "How's my Pet?" Virgie's little brother had died when he was only four months old, a long time

15

ago, so Virgie had always been the baby of the family and her father's favorite.

John Wine was of medium height. He was slightly stooped, with deep-set eyes and dark hair that was beginning to turn gray. Virgie had always loved to run her fingers through his long, dark beard when she sat on his lap. She was almost too old for that now, but she still thought her father was the most wonderful man in the world.

At the table the older girls and Father talked about neighborhood news and the farm work. Pearl was quiet and kept trading glances with Virgie. Once Virgie spoke up, "Lizzie, would you pass the meat?"

"I don't answer to that name and you know it," Elizabeth snapped.

"Oh, I'm sorry, Liz—Elizabeth," Virgie said. "It's hard to remember you want us to say Elizabeth."

"Well, here's the meat," Elizabeth said. Virgie stole a look at Father. He didn't say anything, but she knew it hurt him when they were angry with each other. It hurt her, too, She felt all torn up inside tonight.

Pearl and Virgie went to bed soon after the dishes were done and the evening work was finished. They had to get up early for school and, besides, it seemed to Virgie that Pearl felt as she did, sorry for what they had done and disappointed that Katie didn't have an "understanding."

"I bet Katie feels bad when she hears the other girls talking. Do you think she's going to be an old maid? She's too pretty not to get married," Virgie said.

"Oh, I guess she still has time to get married, but I wanted it to be George, and that letter didn't say a thing. It might as well have been written by Katie's friend Anna for all it said," Pearl replied, brushing her hair.

"Sh-h-h, someone's coming," Virgie whispered.

There was a light knock on the door and Katie entered. She seemed nervous, walking around the room, hanging up clothes and straightening things. Maybe she's found out about the letter, Virgie thought. I wish we hadn't read it.

Finally Katie said, "Do you remember George McKibbin

16

from Kansas? Well, he's coming again. We—we're going to be married!"

Virgie sat down suddenly on the bed. "M-m-married! That—that's wonderful! But—but when did you know? I mean—when did he ask you?" she stuttered.

"Virgie, that's none of our business," Pearl said, but Virgie thought she wanted to know, too.

"Oh, that's all right," Katie laughed. We've been planning it for awhile, but he didn't know when his new job would start down in Otoe County."

"You mean you won't be living at home anymore?" asked Virgie.

"Well, of course not, goosey." replied Pearl.

Virgie blushed. That question really had sounded like a dunce, but somehow she hadn't thought of Katie going away. Katie had been their "mother" for as long as Virgie could remember. What would home be like without her?

Katie pulled the covers tight around both girls and Pearl seemed to go to sleep immediately, but Virgie lay awake a long time. She'd always thought it would be wonderful to be grown up, but today she couldn't play tag when she wanted to and now Katie was getting married and going away and everything was going to be different.

Even after Virgie heard Father come to bed, she couldn't get to sleep. How did Katie know George wanted her to marry him when all he said in the letter was that he bought a new horse? Finally her curiosity got the better of her. She just *had* to look at that letter again. Maybe there was something on the back.

Virgie got out of bed and tiptoed through the hall to the kitchen. A cold moon was shining through the window and she could see the letter on the clock shelf. Virgie took it down, but didn't want to light a lamp. Maybe there was still enough fire in the stove to see by. Lifting off one of the heavy iron stove lids, Virgie took a cob and stirred the coals until they burst into flame.

Holding the letter close to the stove, she was starting to open it when she suddenly saw the postmark: Menlo, Kan-

17

sas, March 16, 1894. That was way last spring! This was
November! This was an old letter that had probably been
on the shelf all summer! Katie could have gotten a dozen
letters since then and she wouldn't have left them around
for little girls to get into.

Giggling to herself, Virgie replaced the stove lid, returned
the letter and tiptoed back to bed, snuggling up next to
Pearl and curling her cold toes inside her long flannel
nightgown. Well, I guess we're two silly little geese, she
thought. After this, we'll wait until Katie tells us what she
wants us to know. But just think what fun it'll be to tell the
girls we're going to have a wedding!

Chapter 3.
KATIE'S WEDDING

Virgie looked at her hands and sighed. She seemed to have more stove blacking on herself than on the stove. She hated to black the stove, but Pearl and Lizzie were cleaning the front room, and Katie was putting the finishing touches on her dress. Virgie sighed again and bent to rub the oven door as hard as she could. Fortunately it wasn't a very cold day, since they had to let the fire go out to polish the stove. After that cold spell they'd had the first of the month it had warmed up.

Virgie and Pearl had stayed home from school today because Katie's wedding was tomorrow. It sure was exciting to have a wedding, but it was a lot of work, too. Just when Katie had been busy getting her things ready, the threshers had come. That had meant big meals for Katie and Lizzie to prepare. Virgie and Pearl had rushed home from school to watch the huge horses going round and round the big circular track, providing power for the machine. The hum of the machinery rose and fell in regular rhythm as the horses moved.

Now as she polished, Virgie tried not to think what life would be like without Katie. She really couldn't imagine it. Mike and David worked away from home and Elizabeth had "worked out" sometimes, but Katie had always been home. Maybe if Virgie thought about George she could forget about Katie's leaving. She'd always liked George, but she hadn't seen him since they left Kansas. She hoped he

19

wouldn't try to hold her on his lap and give her gum the way he used to. After all, she was pretty grown-up now.

Katie came into the kitchen to get a drink from the water bucket sitting on the end of the dry sink. "My, that's a good job, Virgie. The stove never looked nicer."

"Thank you, Katie. I was just thinking about the time in Kansas that you had your bangs in curlers when George stopped by and he teased you so about it. How are you going to wear your hair for the wedding?"

"The same way as always, I guess. I don't want him to think he's marrying a stranger," she joked.

Virgie stood up to rest her aching back. "He'd never think that! Oh, Katie, aren't you excited? How can you just keep on sewing and doing everyday things?"

Katie's curls shook as she laughed. "Because the everyday things are here to be done, I guess." Then she grew sober. "Yes, I am excited, Virgie. I'm excited, and happy, and sad to be leaving all of you, and a little scared, all at once."

Suddenly Virgie could feel the tears coming. "Why, Katie, do you feel that way, too? I—I just can't think what it's going to be like with—without you."

Katie moved swiftly to her, holding Virgie tight. "I know, Pet. It's going to be different. Even though the boys have been working away, this will be more of a break in our family. I thought maybe I shouldn't go now, but Mike and Father think you can get along."

"Oh, we can, Katie. You mustn't give up getting married for us. Pearl and I can do a lot of work after school and on Saturday and Father doesn't have so much to do outside in the winter. He's a good cook. Remember how he used to make Christmas cookies every year when we were little?"

Katie smiled gently. "Yes, I remember. I'm sure you'll get along just fine. I'll write to you, and try to get home every so often." Virgie wiped her eyes with her wrist and backed away.

"Oh, dear, now I've got blacking on you. I've got to finish this up. It's getting chilly in here without a fire. Katie, can I go with Mike and Father to meet George? You know how the blacking smells when we first build a fire."

"Yes, I guess you can," Katie laughed. "You've all helped so well that there isn't much more to do. I think you should go along."

Virgie's hands were almost clean by afternoon. She had scrubbed them until they were sore and only a few black smudges still showed around her nails. Maybe if I wash the dishes tonight they'll really get white, she thought.

She stood beside Father and watched Mike bring up the horses. Mike, twenty-seven, was the oldest of the family. Like the rest of them, he was short and slim, with small facial features and dark hair. He was a hard worker and an excellent horseman. Virgie was never afraid when Mike was driving, no matter how much the horses leaped and pranced. Now he held them steady as she and Father climbed into the wagon. They turned down the lane, lined with mulberry and wild plum trees, and onto the dirt road that ran by the farm and led to Shrevesville.

The horses were big, beautiful sorrels. They had been working hard on the farm, so took their time pulling to the top of the ridge. Virgie looked around with interest. It was more fun to be riding next to Father than walking over this ridge. The November wind whistled through a few dry corn stalks still standing in the fields. At the top of the ridge Virgie looked over into the pasture to see if she could see prairie-dog town, but it was just under the crest of the hill.

Now they were over the ridge and could see the village of Shrevesville laid out in the valley before them. To the right was the school and ahead was Main Street, with the general store and the post office, the blacksmith shop and the Baptist church, all small wooden buildings. The Methodist church and several houses stood back from the street on the left.

The Dunker church, where Virgie's family went, was farther out of town toward the west. Father said the official name of their church was German Baptist Brethren, but among themselves they usually shortened it to Brethren.

21

Many people called it the Dunker church, but Virgie didn't like that name very much. Virgie's friend, Lottie Keller, lived not far from the church, but her house couldn't be seen from town.

Mike flicked the reins. "I hear the Baptist church is talking about getting electric lights. The Methodists down in David City have them and the Baptists want to be first here," he said.

"Yes, I'm afraid worldliness is creeping into the churches," sighed Father. "It don't seem necessary to have such fancy meeting houses."

"That's true," Mike replied, "but trimming all those lamps is sure a big job."

Virgie looked around eagerly as they went through town. School must be out by now, so maybe she would see Dot or Maggie or even Queenie Shay. Of course she wouldn't call out to tell them where she was going, but it would still be nice to have them see her. The streets seemed deserted, however, and soon they were through town and heading downhill toward the Platte Valley.

The Platte River was wide and shallow, with several miles of flat lowlands on each side. Virgie liked to look at the flat land with the river like a ribbon in the center, so different from the hills she knew. The trees were larger here and more plentiful, growing beside the water as well as on the sandbars that rose out of the quiet river.

The horses seemed excited by the water, too. They began to run down the long slope and Mike let them go. Virgie clung to Father tightly, hearing the wind rush past her ears. It made her eyes water so that everything became a blur. She wondered how Mike could see where the road was. After a good run the horses slowed down and Virgie looked eagerly for the rutted section of the valley where the early wagon trails had been. The deep ruts were still not completely covered with grass.

"Were there still wagon trains on the trails when you came out here from Virginia in '76, Father?" she asked.

"Yes. It wasn't unusual to see covered wagons or freight

22

wagon goin' through, 'specially if they was headed for places where the railroad wasn't finished yet."

"But there weren't many roads, were there?"

"No. When we got off the train up here at Rogers Station, there was no one to meet us, so we set off with the children along a cow path through slough grass eight feet tall,"
Father recounted.

"I remember that," Mike offered. "I was nine when we
came and the grass was way over my head. It was like going
through a tunnel."

"Did you live there before you moved to Risings?" Virgie
asked, watching the river come nearer as they approached
it.

"We lived right at the edge of the bluffs, so we could look
down on the Platte bottoms," Father replied.

"We've been learning about the river in school. Did you
know Platte is a French word that means shallow water?"

"Is it now, Pet? Well, if that don't beat the Dutch," Father exclaimed.

They were approaching the bridge now. It looked to Virgie as if it stretched endlessly ahead across the wide water.
She knew she wasn't going to fall off the open wagon seat,
but still she leaned closer to Father. It seemed like such a
short drop over the wagon side, under the bridge railing and
into the water beneath.

"Goodness, how long is this bridge, Mike?"

"Three-quarters of a mile."

"How long has it been since it went out?"

"Oh, several years. I s'pose it's about time for it to go out
again," Mike replied teasingly.

"Oh-oh-oh," shivered Virgie.

"Now, Virgie, you know that only happens in the spring
when the ice piles up against the supports. It's not even frozen over today."

Just the same, Virgie was relieved when they were back
on dry land and rolling toward Schuyler, where George
would be coming on the four fifty-nine train. Soon she
could see the buildings of the town, with hills rising again in

23

the distance. Father pulled out his big watch as they drove up to the railroad station.

"We timed it just right, Mike. It's four thirty-five."

Mike stayed with the horses, but Virgie was glad to stretch her legs as she walked with Father on the platform. It was fun to watch the small groups of people waiting for the train, the Carts loaded with baggage, the stray dogs and townspeople who appeared whenever a train was due. They came down the dirt street from town, past the hotel, the livery stable and some buildings used for storage. Virgie watched some women holding up their long skirts as they carefully crossed the dirty street.

They heard the whistle and soon the train came into view. Virgie drew back as the huge puffing engine approached the platform. There was a screaming of brakes and a noisy jolt jarred through each car as the train stopped. The engine panted and hissed.

Virgie eagerly watched the people getting off, hoping to be the first to see George. She'd know him by his mustache, she knew. A young couple with a baby got off and were met by an older couple, probably their parents. Some traveling salesmen appeared with their valises at the top of the steps. Two bags of mail were given to the station agent. Then the conductor started taking tickets from people who were boarding the train.

"Father, where's George?" Virgie asked worriedly. "Isn't this the train he was coming on?"

"I thought so, Pet," Father said soberly.

"Bo-o-o-ard," the conductor shouted. The engine puffed a little faster and the train began to move. Virgie and Father slowly walked back to where Mike held the horses, Virgie looking around anxiously to see if they had missed George.

"Well, I don't understand it, but maybe Katie didn't get the time right," said Pa.

"There's not another train till tonight. We can't wait that long," replied Mike.

"No, we'll just have to go back. If he's brave enough to

24

marry in these hard times I guess he can take care of his-self," grinned Father.

Virgie didn't think it was funny. Whatever would they tell Kate? She was getting a big supper ready. What if something had happened to George? Virgie couldn't bear to think of Katie's being disappointed.

"I was talking to an emigrant from North Dakota while you were at the depot," Mike said, as the horses trotted back toward the river. "He was headin' for Oklahoma terri-tory. He said wheat got only ten inches high last summer and the best of it only made two bushels to the acre. Said it's been six years since they had a good crop."

Father sighed. "Between the Panic and the drought we're sure having a rough time. I feel for these poor emi-grant families, leaving wherever they were and not knowin' where they're goin' or if things'll be better when they get there. It's hard enough here, but I believe it's better to stay than to drift around. Still, it's hard to tell. I sometimes wonder if we shoulda let the homestead go."

Usually the talk about prices, crops and drought worried Virginia, but today she was too concerned about George and Katie to listen. The ride to Schuyler had taken a long time, but Virgie wished the trip home would take even longer, so she wouldn't have to see Katie's face.

When they did tell Katie, she just said quietly, "Well, I guess he'll come tomorrow." But her mouth shut a little tighter and Virgie was sure she looked pale. They went ahead with the evening work, but everyone seemed espe-cially quiet.

"Oh, Virgie," whispered Pearl, as they were getting ready for bed, "wouldn't it be just awful if George wouldn't come at all? Maggie Peterson told me about that happening to someone her mother knew."

"Don't say it, Pearl! I know George wouldn't do that to Katie! He couldn't! I just hope he isn't sick or something."

The wedding day dawned bright and clear, with crisp sunshine. The wedding was planned for one o'clock, so there'd be plenty of time for Katie and George to make the afternoon train. Everyone went ahead with the preparations as if they knew George was coming, but Virgie caught Katie glancing anxiously out the window several times.

At ten o'clock Virgie went in to dust the front room, in case it had gotten dirty since yesterday. All at once she heard the dog barking, a commotion outside and then voices. Bursting out of the room, she flung open the kitchen door and there was George, with Katie and Pearl, and Lizzie running up from the barn.

Virgie was so happy for Katie that she felt limp. She wanted to rush out toward them, but shyness held her back. She clung to the kitchen doorknob, watching them come toward the house, all talking at once.

"You mean you were there to meet me yesterday?" George asked. "Pshaw, that's too bad. Your folks must have been waiting on the depot side. I didn't expect anyone to meet me, so I got off on the other side of the train and went to the hotel. I thought I'd just wait till this morning and then hire a rig and come out."

When they came to the doorstep the girls went on into the house, but George stopped beside Virgie. His brown eyes twinkled above his big mustache just as she remembered. "Hello, there, Virgie. My, aren't you getting grown up! Do you still like gum?"

"I—I guess so," Virgie stammered, wishing she could think of something ladylike to say. George laughed, tweaked her braid lightly and stepped into the house.

Then all was excitement, for there was another surprise when Father and Mike came into dinner. David was with them! David had worked away from home almost since Virgie could remember, and she hardly knew him. He was only two years younger than Katie. When they were little they must have been good chums, like Pearl and I are, Virgie thought. It seemed strange to think her grownup brothers and sisters had once been little children.

"Why, David, did you leave your work just to come to my wedding?" asked Katie. David hugged her.

"Well, now, I couldn't let my big sister get married without me, could I?" he asked. "We've been working pretty long hours in the print shop, but Mr. Knuttleman said he could let me off today, so I hitched a ride on a freight wagon as far as David City, and then came on up this morning."

Virgie looked at David, trying to memorize his face, since she didn't see him often. He had the same high forehead as the rest of the family, with bushy eyebrows over his blue eyes. His light, wavy hair was parted in the middle and he was the tallest of the family. Once he winked at Virgie and she grinned back, a warm feeling spreading through her.

Then they all went to dress. Virgie finished first and stole back to the kitchen to see that everything was cleared away. George was standing at the window.

"Do you remember when I used to come to the sod house in Kansas and get Katie?" he asked.

"Yes, of course I do."

"What did she say when I didn't come yesterday?"

"She didn't say much, but I knew she didn't like it."

There was a knock at the door and Virgie opened it to Brother Hersler, the minister. He shook hands with George and talked soberly to other members of the family as they came in. Suddenly Virgie felt very solemn.

Soon everyone went quietly into the front room where the sun was shining through the yellowed lace curtains onto the horsehair sofa. Virgie and Pearl squeezed into the big chair, holding each others' hands tightly. The minister stood behind the heavy oak library table which held the family Bible and some dried strawflowers.

Katie and George took their places facing Brother Hersler. Katie's dress was a lovely soft brown sateen, which shimmered in the sunlight. The tight bodice was made with many tucks and a high, standing collar. The sleeves were tightly fitted, but the long skirt hung full and heavy to the floor. Virgie noticed that Katie's head tilted to the left as she listened. George seemed to look at the floor all during the long service.

Then it was over, and everyone was laughing, crying, hugging, kissing all at once. Pearl and Virgie helped Katie

27

put the last of her things in her trunk. Mike brought up the horse and buggy George had rented at the livery stable. David and Father helped load everything in.

"Is this your address, Katie, when I want to write to you?" Virgie asked.

Katie took the paper on which was written "Mrs. George McKibbin, Douglas, Otoe County, Nebraska." "Mrs. George McKibbin! My goodness, is that me? No one's ever called me that before. Yes, I guess that's right. Be sure to write me all the news!"

There was a last round of good-byes, and George helped Katie into the buggy. The family stood nd waved as they drove out the lane and turned onto the road, but suddenly Virgie couldn't see at all. She turned to run into the house and bumped squarely into David. He caught her in his arms.

"Hey, little sister, where're you going?" Noticing the tears on her lashes, he said quietly, "I know it hurts to have her go, Virgie, but I'll be here until tomorrow. Won't that help a little?"

"Oh, will you, David?" Virgie rubbed her eyes with her hand. "Will you tell me all about your work and the people you know, the way you used to when you'd come home? Remember how you used to come home from building the railroad in Kansas and tell me stories?"

David laughed. "Yes, I'll see what wonderful stories I can tell." Together they walked into the house.

Chapter 4.
SPRING FUN

"Oh, Pearl, is there anything better than spring? Just feel that air and look at those billowy clouds up there, blowing across the sky like the tumbleweeds used to bounce across the prairie in Kansas. Isn't it wonderful to know that winter is about over?" exclaimed Virgie, as she shifted her books and lunch pail to the other arm.

Pearl coughed as she stepped carefully over the stream of melted snow water running down the middle of the road. "Yes, it's good to know that summer's coming."

Virgie looked at her anxiously. Pearl had never seemed too well and this last winter had been even harder on her than usual. The girls had missed Katie more than they'd ever dreamed. They'd had no idea there was so much work to keeping house. Father had been wonderful help, but still there was always so much to do after school. Sometimes they tried to do more in the mornings, but then they had to run all the way to school to be on time. When they arrived Pearl would be so faint that Virgie would have to fan her awhile in the cloakroom before they could go in.

Virgie had thought several times that Elizabeth could have been a great deal more help, but she preferred working outside. Even when Lizzie was in the house, she never saw anything to do, and it was easier to do the work than to argue about it. Many times that winter Virgie had remembered wistfully how much easier everything had been when Katie was home, but she always felt ashamed for thinking it, because Katie was so happy in her new home.

29

Today, though, no one could be sad with that wonderful April air all around. Virgie felt like skipping and turning cartwheels all the way home. Suddenly she stopped.

"Look, Pearl. See how the snow melts next to the ground, so there's a cunning little shelf of snow sticking out over the water. Wouldn't it be fun to go wading?"

"Oh, Virgie! It makes me shiver to think of it. But let's do!"

"Pearl! You mean it? It would be so foolish, but what fun! Come on. I'll race you to the house!"

Flying down the hill, the girls rushed into the kitchen and flung their books on the table. On the stove stood a pot of partially cooked beans.

"See what Father did? He must have known we'd want to play a little today. I'll build up the fire and get the beans cooking again," said Pearl.

In a few minutes the girls were outside again, standing at the edge of the draw that ran beside the house. It was a steep ravine, with muddy banks where the snow had melted. Pearl and Virgie took off their shoes and stockings, held up their skirts and slid down the steep muddy sides to the bottom of the draw. The sun couldn't reach the bottom, where there was still a lot of snow, but in the middle the running water gurgled cheerfully.

Virgie stepped carefully over the snow bank into the running water. "O-o-o-h-h-h, Pearl, it's so cold! It's terrible! But it's so much fun. Come on!"

Gasping, Pearl also stepped into the icy water. With squeals and giggles the girls waded until their teeth were chattering and their feet had turned blue. Then they clambered out and up the muddy bank again, arriving at the top quite bedraggled.

"I can't race you this time," Pearl said. "My feet are too numb to feel anything, so I have to watch where I'm going."

At the doorstep the girls washed and dried their muddy feet. In the kitchen they pulled two chairs up to the open oven door and put their feet as far into the oven as they dared, letting the delicious warmth soak into their very bones. The pot of beans bubbled noisily and filled the room with a wonderful aroma.

"This is wonderful," sighed Pearl. "Why don't we just sit here for a month?"

Virgie stretched.

"Then we'd miss Arbor Day and May Day and my birthday," she said practically. "Isn't it nice to have so many things happening after such a long, dull winter?"

"Mr. Mason says the legislature has decided to nickname Nebraska 'The Tree Planters' State' because we were the first to celebrate Arbor Day," reported Pearl.

"I know. Way back in 1872 it was suggested by Mr. J. Sterling Morton. Isn't that a name to roll under your tongue? J. Sterling Morton!" Virginia said.

Pearl stretched and yawned. "Well, these special days can't come too soon for me. But right now we'd better get out of these muddy clothes if we're going to have supper ready for Father, Mike and Elizabeth. They'll be tired and hungry."

Arbor Day was bright and windy. There was an undercurrent of excitement in school. When Virgie's assignments were finished, she practiced writing her name: "Miss Virginia May Wine, April 20, 1895." She wasn't sure why they were all going to put their names in a bottle and plant it with the tree, but she wasn't going to ask. She could just see how Queenie Shay would laugh and toss her head at such a dumb question.

At last, everyone marched out to the corner of the schoolyard. There Mr. Mason gave a talk about how important trees were. As he rambled on, Virgie's thoughts wandered. Father said that in the East—Ohio and Virginia—trees grew everywhere without any help and the first thing the settlers had to do was cut them down. Surely those people couldn't have the same feeling for trees as we do, Virgie thought. Here a tree is something to be cherished and watched and cared for. That's why we never throw out any water in dry weather, but always put it on the trees. That's why the cottonwood grove beside our sod shanty in Kansas meant so much to us. I remember how their glossy leaves shone like satin in the sun.

Suddenly a trio of older girls was singing "Welcome, Sweet Springtime." As she listened Virgie watched a hawk sailing on the wind far, far up in a sky so blue it hurt to look at it. Then it was time for the planting. Pearl dropped the bottle containing everyone's names into the hole. The older boys carefully set a young box elder tree into the hole they had dug earlier and filled in the dirt around it, placing a circle of wire around it for protection. Then everyone sang "America" and walked back to the schoolhouse, thinking soberly that they had contributed to the future.

The first day of May ended with a balmy spring evening. In the cloudless sky the evening star hung like a beacon above the spot where the sun had set. Virgie lingered outside as long as she could, almost aching because it was so beautiful, but as twilight settled, she reluctantly turned back to the house and the supper dishes. As she poured water from the teakettle into the dishpan, she remembered the whisperings she'd heard at school that day about May baskets.

It was fun to make May baskets, gathering bits of ribbon, hunting spring flowers in the pasture, using pretty picture cards, making a basket from paper or using one carefully saved from another year. The idea was to arrange as pretty a basket as possible, hang it quietly on the doorknob of a friend's house, knock, then run quickly and hide before the door was opened. But, living out on the farm, there was no one close enough. Town children could slip out and hang baskets and still return before too late.

Today at school she'd heard whispers, though. It seemed the boys were always nudging Henry Nellman when she looked their way. She'd noticed Henry watching her a few times, but he'd never spoken directly to her. Maybe he's as shy as I am, Virgie thought.

As it grew darker Father and Mike came into the house

32

and Father settled down to the sock he was knitting. He wanted to finish another pair before summer came. Elizabeth was staying at the neighbor's, "helping out" since Mrs. Smithton had her baby. Virgie and Pearl finished the dishes and settled down to study.

Suddenly Buster, the dog, began a loud barking. He was a good watchdog and didn't bark without reason, so they knew someone was outside. Mike opened the door and Virgie peeked from behind him. Against the fading western light, she could just see some figures in the lane.

"Who is it?" Mike called.

"Just some fellers," a voice answered. Virgie's heart beat faster. She knew that was Henry's voice.

"I guess they're hanging May baskets," she said. To her surprise Mike didn't call Buster, so he kept on barking threateningly. Disappointed, Virgie watched Mike close the door and sit down again. After awhile Buster's barking faded, but there was no quiet knock on the door.

Virgie's head was in a whirl. She didn't know if she were glad or sorry Henry hadn't left the basket. Would Henry think she didn't like him, since Mike hadn't called the dog? Why should Mike keep her from having a May basket? No, that didn't make sense! Virgie sighed. It wasn't Mike's fault that Henry was afraid of Buster. She was as mixed up as smearcase and apple butter, as Father would say.

Next day the whole school was full of reports of May baskets hung and received. Queenie Shay had been *very* daring and had hung one for Mr. Mason, but he'd been away and his landlady had answered Queenie's knock. Maggie and Dot thought it served Queenie right for being so bold.

Then Dot turned to Virgie. "Oh, Virgie, you surely missed a lovely basket, with purple ribbons and candy and everything. My brother Rolf told me all about it. Henry Nellman fixed it and I know he meant it for you, but I didn't understand why they didn't leave it."

"I guess we live too far out," Virgie said practically. Somehow she didn't want to explain what had happened. It was enough to know that Henry had made it for her.

Virgie felt it was going to be a good summer. In a couple weeks she'd be a whole year older. Surely then she'd be able to think of clever things to say. She wouldn't be shy anymore. She and Pearl would do a better job of keeping house when school was out and she could work on feeling kinder toward everyone, the way Sister Miller was always telling them in Sunday School. Yes, it was going to be a good summer.

Chapter 5.
SINGING SCHOOL

It was a growing-up summer—with work! Virgie wondered many times how Katie had done it all. In addition to carrying water from the windmill and doing the washing and the housework, there was always the next meal to plan and prepare. Elizabeth was "working out" almost all the time now, so Virgie and Pearl were home alone.

Father and Mike worked very hard in the fields, so it was the girls' job to care for the baby chicks. The hens had been set in the spring, before school was out. As the chicks hatched they were placed in a box beneath the stove until they were warm and dry. When the days grew warmer, each hen and her chicks were moved outside to individual coops built like an "A". Slats across the front kept the hen in but allowed the chicks to run.

There was constant danger from chicken hawks. They seemed to sail lazily through the blue sky, but were quick to swoop down on a wandering young chicken. The captive hens clucked warningly when the hawks' shadows passed over, and the baby chicks hid instantly. The penned-up hens had to be fed, the chicks were always tipping or dirtying their water pans, and the awkward, heavy coops had to be moved to new locations several times a week.

Virgie had always enjoyed summer and caring for the chicks, but this year something was wrong. She'd thought it would be a good summer, but was this all there was? Was being fourteen just this hard, hard work that wore her down until all she could do was fall into bed at night so she could work again the next day? If only something *exciting* would happen!

Virgie didn't know what she wanted, but it was more than she had. She'd thought her birthday would make a difference, but everything was just the same. She was still shy little Virgie. When are people going to call me Virginia? she wondered.

Father was a wonderful gardener. Even in the dry years he had a better garden than anyone else. He worked such long hours in the field that Virgie tried to help him in the evenings, even though she longed to sit down and rest. As long as there was water in the draw, they carried dripping buckets to the young plants. And there was always hoeing. Virgie could never understand why the weeds grew so well when the plants didn't.

In spite of her aching muscles Virgie enjoyed the evenings with Father while Mike was doing chores and Pearl was finishing up in the house. She loved to watch the swallows fly in and out of the barn, dipping and wheeling as they snapped at insects. And there were nearly always brilliant sunsets painting the clouds with glorious colors, then fading slowly until stars appeared in the velvety sky and it was too dark to see the plants underfoot.

Sometimes Virgie thought she couldn't stand such beauty. If there were only someone she could share her feelings with! She loved Father dearly, and she knew he loved her, but now he was too tired to joke and have fun as they did on long winter evenings. Besides, Father was old and surely wouldn't understand. Pearl was a dear sister, but she needed to rest. She was usually in bed when Virgie and Father finally went to the house. And Mike was so much older. Virgie was afraid he would tease, and that would be worse than keeping her thoughts locked up inside. Wasn't there someone, somewhere, she could talk to?

Just before school started again, David came home with

a surprise. He was giving up his job in the printing office at Papillion and was going to get a farm job in the neighborhood. Even when he stayed at his work-home during the week he would be home on Saturday evening and Sunday.

It was a new experience to have another big brother at home. It soon proved to be a wonderful one. David was just ten years older than Virgie, so she felt he was very wise and experienced.

It was fun to have David around, too, because he liked to go places at night and he thought Virgie was old enough to go along, much to her delight. David was a natural leader, with his good looks, enthusiasm and ability. Thanks to him, Virgie and Pearl were invited to join the Literary Society, which met on Saturday nights, and the Musical Union.

The Union had been organized by the community young people and met at the Baptist church. Professor Glade came on the train from Fremont College to conduct the class. He had been educated at some conservatory in the East and the members of the Musical Union often told themselves how fortunate they were to have contact with such a cultured person. He was a short, distinguished-looking man with a gray goatee, artistic hands and a sensitive face.

Virgie felt very shy and out of place the first time she went to a rehearsal. She had a clear, true soprano voice and loved to sing, but she was sure she'd do some silly thing that would make David sorry he had brought her.

When they entered the church, Virgie was relieved to see Lottie Keller among the young people from the Brethren church. Their families had been friends for many years. Lottie was a year older than Virgie, but this summer Virgie had been promoted to the next older Sunday School class, so now she and Lottie were together. Lottie had quit school when she finished the sixth reader, so they could see each other only at church and evening meetings. Now Lottie broke away from the group and smilingly came to greet Virgie.

37

"I'm so glad you came, Virgie. You sing so well that this'll be jolly fun for you." Virgie looked around anxiously.

"But I don't know where to go or what to do."

"Well, you just sit with me tonight. We'd better sit down. Professor Glade expects to start right on time and makes us pay strict attention."

Virgie dodged a large moth flying around the lamp.

"I just feel like such a dunce. I've never done this before."

Lottie smoothed out her skirt.

"Didn't you ever read the Rudiments of Music at the beginning of our hymn book when the sermon was long? This is pretty much like that. You're so clever, you'll catch on quickly."

Virgie was shocked. She didn't know anyone else spent boring sermon hours reading the front of *The Brethren's Hymnal.* If only she could remember what it said! Peeking at the music Professor Glade was passing out, Virgie saw that the notes looked the same—squares, triangles, diamonds and other queer shapes, but she had never understood them very well. And what were those strange names for them? Suddenly Virgie wished she could run home, but everyone was seated and quiet, so she couldn't leave without being noticed.

"Let's begin with some scales," said Professor Glade, tapping his tuning fork.

"Do, re, mi, fa, sol, la, ti, do" the group sang. "Do," Professor Glade sang, a half step higher, and again the scale rolled out. Goodness, how wonderful it sounds, Virgie thought. They sang several scales and Virgie could almost get the syllables in the right order. Then suddenly they were going down, "Do, ti, la, sol, fa, mi, re, do." Virgie's tongue couldn't get anything right. How did they know he was going down? she thought. He must have given a down signal when I was watching that moth fly into the lamp. Everyone's laughing! But maybe they're laughing at themselves. I wasn't the only one who missed.

Again the professor gave the pitch, but then he suddenly said "Sol." Immediately the group answered, singing the correct note. "Mi", and they responded. "La" was harder and several voices wavered, as they struggled to find the right place. Oh, I'll never get it, Virgie thought. But isn't it fun!

"Cadences," said the Professor, assigning pitches to each part. "Do, sol, mi, do." What a good, solid chord it was! Suddenly the professor moved his hand. The basses, tenors, altos changed their pitch and there was another wonderful chord. Again a flick of the wrist and everyone seemed to know just what pitch to sing, although Virgie realized the sopranos had gone down to "ti" and she was still on "do." Then another signal and the original chord was back, strong and firm. Virgie was covered with goose bumps. She knew some of the older members of the Dunker church felt everyone should sing the tune, but how could anything so beautiful be wrong? Surely those last chords had rolled right up to heaven.

Then they opened the books. Virgie had never followed the notes very much at church, since she knew the familiar tunes. The Dunker congregation was so used to the "old" book, which had only words, that they sang many different hymns to the same tune. Virgie knew that Elder Peters had been opposed to buying the new "worldly" books, but since they only sang the same hymns they'd sung before, she couldn't see that it made so much difference.

Now she realized that they were expected to tell what pitch to sing from the shape of the note. The round one with one side cut off was "do", the diamond shape was "mi", the square was "la." Oh, dear! Would she ever learn? By this time Virgie saw that she wasn't the only one in trouble, and she was trying so hard that she stopped thinking of herself. Just as she was beginning to think it was making a little sense, Professor Glade stopped them.

"I think you've done very well for the first session," he said. "I'm sure what you learned last spring will come back to you before too long and we can go on to new material. That will be all for tonight."

"Now, that wasn't so bad, was it, Virgie?" Lottie asked when they were dismissed.

"Oh, it was wonderful," Virgie sighed. "I just hope I can learn fast enough not to make a goose of myself."

As they were leaving the church Virgie overheard one of the Baptist men say, "We almost have enough money in the fund to order our piano."

"Is that so?" asked David.

"Yes, we've been working at it for a long time. I hear the Methodists down in David City are talking about an organ, but I guess a piano will have to do for us."

Virgie's heart sank. A piano in the church? That would be sinful! She knew Baptists didn't believe like Brethren, but surely they knew pianos and organs were for dance music and theaters. Of course, Queenie Shay had a reed organ in her home, but Virgie couldn't imagine an instrument in church!

As they walked home in the crisp October night, Pearl and David talked about who had been at rehearsal until Virgie broke in with a troubled voice.

"David, if the Baptists get a piano, those of us from the Dunker church won't be allowed to go to Musical Union, will we? I just couldn't stand it not to go anymore." Virgie stumbled over a stone in the dark and David caught her arm.

"Let's not worry about it too soon," he reassured her. "The Baptists haven't gotten it yet. And if there's too much criticism we can probably move our rehearsals to some other place." Virgie was unconvinced.

"That part singing we were doing tonight was so beautiful! I don't see how it could be wrong, but I know Elder Peters wouldn't like it."

"I know we must respect our elders," Pearl spoke up, "but I don't believe part singing is so bad. You know our new hymn books have four-part music. I'm sure Annual

40

Meeting wouldn't have let The Brethren's Publishing Company print the books if it were so wrong."

David opened a gate, so they could cut across the cornfield. "I think it's like this, Virgie," he said seriously. "God made me a man and gave me a man's voice," David made his voice all deep and hollow. "So why should I sing praises to God, like the Psalms say, with a high, screechy woman's voice?" He made his voice go high and scratchy and the girls giggled.

"Besides," David continued. "I read in *The Gospel Messenger* that two of the young leaders of our church, Brother Holsinger and Brother Showalter, say church music should be improved and are holding singing schools themselves. They're good musicians, so surely they must be teaching part singing."

"You don't think Dunkers will ever have musical instruments in church, do you?" asked Pearl.

"Oh, no, I don't think we'll ever go that far," David answered as they reached the farmyard.

Before she got into bed, Virgie stood at her window. The stars seeemed almost close enough to touch. When she looked up the ravine she could see lights from Lottie's house. It was so wonderful to have a friend like Lottie! And now Musical Union! There may be a lot of work to growing-up, but these extra things are almost worth it, she decided.

Chapter 6.
REVIVAL MEETING

"Anyone here want to go to meeting tonight?" David asked when he suddenly appeared at the door as the family was sitting around the supper table.

Pearl rose and started to set another place. "Why, David, where did you come from? Have you eaten?" she asked.

"Yes, we ate. We got the last of the fodder hauled today and Mr. Wrightsman said I could have the evening off if I wanted to go to church. Since I took him at his word, I guess I'd better show up," David grinned.

Mike and Father had chores to finish, and Pearl needed to study. But Virgie decided to go. There was only a little snow on the ground when Virgie and David started. The cold January wind that had chased her and Pearl home from school had died down, leaving clear skies and glittering, distant stars. The snow crunched beneath their feet and their breath hung in the air.

It was almost too cold to talk, so Virgie looked up at David and thought how lucky she was that this wonderful, big brother had come back to work near home. She had discovered that he never laughed at her ideas, but listened as if they were important. He talked to her as Virgie thought a mother would talk to her daughter, and some of the loneliness in her heart was beginning to disappear.

The Brethren church was only a mile and a half from the farm, so they arrived during the song service. As they approached the old schoolhouse which the Brethren used for a church, Virgie could tell they were "lining" the hymns. There was a pause after each line while the song leader recited the words for the next line.

"Oh, why are they doing it that old-fashioned way?" she asked impatiently. "Why don't they use our new books?"

David stamped the snow from his shoes. "Well, you know the evangelist is quite old. Maybe he's like Elder Peters and thinks the old ways are better. I guess we can do it this way once without hurting us," he replied as he opened the door.

"O come, thou wounded Lamb of God," Brother Miller was reciting, and the congregation sang the line. Well, at least Brother Miller has a good voice and never lets us slow down, Virgie thought. As she looked around for Lottie, David slipped his hand under her elbow and guided her down the aisle. Why, he's seating me just like the "paired off" couples, she realized. What a thrill! I hope everyone notices how elegant he looks in his Prince Albert suit.

"Give us to know thy love, then pain," sang the congregation while David and Virgie made their way along the bench. "Is sweet, and life or death is gain," chanted Brother Miller. What's sweet? Virgie wondered. If I had the book I could see what I was singing about instead of being stopped every line. I wonder what Brother Peters would say if I opened the book and tried to figure out the syllables as we sang.

The service continued with more hymns, several Scripture readings and long prayers by each minister present. The oily smell of kerosene lamps filled the air. One of them began burning too high and smoked the chimney. Lottie's father, Jerry Keller, moved quietly to turn it down. During the last hymn before the sermon, two men got up to put more coal in the heating stove. They tried to move quietly, but the clattering and banging almost drowned out the singing.

Then everyone settled down expectantly for the sermon. This evangelist was known to be a "live wire", and tonight there was a fervor of excitement in the room. Soon "Amen" was heard from every corner as members of the congregation approved the minister's words. The sermon became more intense, listing the dangers of ignoring Christ's call or delaying one's acceptance. Even the young men from the community, whom Virgie sometimes thought came just to make fun, seemed to be listening intently.

Virgie had never thought personally about joining the church. She knew Brethren did not approve of infant baptism as the Methodists did, but believed people should wait until they could understand what they were doing. Usually people didn't join until after they were married, and Father was the only one in their family who belonged to the church. Virgie had always assumed that if Mike, David and Katie weren't old enough, surely no one expected her to join. Tonight though she began to feel that perhaps she shouldn't wait on them. The minister was saying that everyone had to accept his own responsibility and couldn't hide behind someone else.

Virgie was testing this new idea when the invitation was given. Well, of course, she couldn't do anything tonight. She'd have to think about it awhile. Besides, she could *never* get up in front of all those people and walk down the aisle, she thought, as she noticed several people around her doing. Just the idea made Virgie shake.

Now Brother Miller announced a familiar hymn from the book so the congregation could sing without interruption. The ministers each went to pray or speak with someone. The singing, the murmuring voices, the soft sound of weeping added to the high feeling in the church.

Suddenly there was a kind of gasp. Virgie stole a glance behind her and saw Alice Streeter coming down the aisle. Virgie's hands grew cold and her throat tightened right in the middle of a word. Alice was Lottie's grown sister. She was married to John Streeter, the community infidel! Would John let her join the church when he didn't even believe in God?

Virgie didn't want to look at Lottie. She was sure the whole family would be in tears, as many others were. Just as Virgie thought she couldn't stand any more excitement, the evangelist closed the meeting, although some would stay to pray with the new converts. The people left the church quietly, but outside there were murmurs and questions about what would happen as a result of Alice's action.

As they stood at the door, Virgie suddenly found herself beside Lottie. She wished so much that she could think of the right thing to say. There weren't any words, though, so she squeezed Lottie's hand and kissed her wet cheek quickly. Lottie gave her a tearful smile and went out the door with her mother.

Virgie was glad for the cold, clear air and the silence broken only by their feet on the crunching snow as she and David walked home. Her head was aching and she felt as if there were a whirlwind inside her. If she'd known the evening was going to be like this, she wouldn't have come. And yet, was this part of growing up, too? Singing school and going places with David were so much fun, and the housework didn't seem so hard to get done anymore. But probably you had to think about serious things, too. You just couldn't have a lark all the time.

"Do you think John will let Alice be baptized?" Virgie asked timidly when she couldn't stay silent anymore. "The Bible says women should obey their husbands, but it also says everyone must answer to God, so what will Alice do?"

"I don't know," David replied seriously. "I guess this just shows how important it is not to marry an unbeliever."

Alice didn't belong to the church when she married John, Virgie thought. Now she's changed and John hasn't. How can people tell if someone will change after they're married? What if you married someone who thought as you did, then found they'd changed after it was too late? Oh, it was too confusing! Virgie's head started to throb again. David paused at the back step.

"Well, here you are home again, Virgie. Thanks for going with me."

"Can't you come in and warm up before you go over to Wrightman's?" Virgie asked as David opened the door.

"If I come in I'll stay too long and there's work tomor-

45

row, so I'd better go on," he said, closing the door. Warmth from the dying fire closed around Virgie.

Father called from his bedroom. "Is that you, Pet? Be sure to warm your feet good before you go to bed."

I'm all mixed up, and all Father cares about is warm feet! Virgie thought. And why does he always call me by that baby name? My name's Virginia! No, that isn't fair. It isn't Father's fault that I have all these queer feelings or that I'm asking questions no one can answer. Father loves me. I just wish I could be a little girl again, so the grown-ups could tell me everything I don't know. I thought I'd learn everything as I grew older, but it seems I know less and less. Sighing, Virgie carried the lamp to her room.

Chapter 7.
SUNDAY AFTERNOONS

Virgie must not have warmed her feet well enough, for in a few days she was down with a feverish cold and a hacking cough. Father made her drink cup after cup of hot salvia tea. Pearl brought her books home from school and Virgie tried to study as she rested on the daybed beside the kitchen stove. She did as much housework as she could, so Pearl wouldn't have so much to do in the evening, but Father didn't like it if he came in at noon and found her up.

Father and Pearl attended more of the revival meetings and reported there had been more converts. Baptismal services were to be on Sunday in the Platte River. The community was still buzzing about Alice Streeter and there were all sorts of rumors about what John would do.

"What makes people think John is an infidel? Did he say he doesn't believe in God?" Virgie asked, as she, Mike and Father ate dinner one sunny day during a sudden January thaw.

"I dunno how the rumor got started, but John's never denied it and you know the Good Book says everyone must witness for Christ or He won't plead for us in the last day," said Father soberly. Virgie squirmed. She didn't want to think about each person's responsibility.

Mike speared another slice of bread with his fork. "Since it's thawing today I wonder how much ice there'll be on the river by Sunday," he mused. Virgie shivered as she thought

47

of walking into the icy river, forgetting how she and Pearl had waded in the melting snow water just last April.

"How can anyone even think of being baptized in the middle of the winter? Surely God doesn't ask people to risk their lives!" she exclaimed, passing the beans to Father.

"The first Dunker baptisms in America were on Christmas day," Father said seriously. "No one's ever gotten sick from being baptized in the winter."

There was a queer look on Mike's face and Virgie wanted to laugh, but choked it back. Father really believed that! Someone must have gotten a cold once, but she mustn't make fun of Father's beliefs.

The whole family wanted to go on Sunday afternoon. Virgie insisted she was quite able to stay by herself, but it did seem a long time till they returned. She anxiously watched the sunlight creep across the wide boards of the kitchen floor and wondered what was happening at the river. Had John and Alice had many quarrels about Alice's decision? Had he let her come? Would she come with the Kellers? Would John come and take her away before it was her turn? The whole family would be so upset. Virgie realized her imagination was running away with her, and tried to concentrate on the Sunday School lesson she'd missed, but she was relieved to finally hear the rattle of harness in the yard.

"What happened? Tell me quick!" she implored, when the family came in.

"Nothing happened," said Pearl casually, a teasing smile on her face.

"Oh, don't torment me. Please tell me!" Virgie begged.

Father emptied the cob basket into the cookstove. "John brought Alice to the river himself," he said. "He watched everything closely and it seemed to make a real impression on him."

Virgie was a little disappointed. "Didn't he make a scene?"

"He just stood there like anyone else. I don't see what all the fuss is about," said Elizabeth, who was home for a few hours from the place where she was "working out." The family Elizabeth worked for was not sympathetic to church, and she had not attended any of the revival meetings.

David had also come home with the family. "Say, Virgie, I almost forgot to tell you about Literary last night," he said now.

"Oh, yes, David. What was the program last night? It wasn't the spelling bee, was it?" Virgie loved spelling bees. The only time she'd ever been spelled down was on the word "poultice."

Elizabeth snorted. "Dot Burden recited 'Curfew Must Not Ring Tonight' and she didn't do nearly as well as you did years ago at Literary in Kansas. Remember?"

"They had a debate on 'The Right and Wrong of Hanging as a Means of Capital Punishment.' Mr. Mason was really good. Almost all the girls were crying before he finished," Pearl added.

Suddenly Virgie realized they were all home but Katie. It had been a long time since the whole family had been together, even though Elizabeth and David worked right in the community.

Virgie looked around at them enjoying the corn Father was popping and thought how lucky she was to have such a family. If only Katie could be here, but, of course, she couldn't come, since little Frank was only a few months old. She wished Douglas weren't so far away. By the time she saw Frank he wouldn't be a baby any more.

"Virgie, I don't think you're listening," David was saying. Everyone thought your rhymes in the Literary paper were very clever and talented. They want something different now and Queenie Shay said you could do it." At the mention of Queenie something snapped in Virgie.

"Oh, I just bet!" she said sarcastically. "I can just hear Queenie saying, 'Why not get little Virgie to do something. She's so clever!' I wish people would stop calling me Virgie! My name's Virginia!"

Father and David looked at her quickly and Virgie was

49

ashamed. What's the matter with me? A minute ago I was so happy with the family and now I'm biting their heads off. Why am I so contented one minute and so snappy the next?

But Elizabeth said practically, "Well, if you want people to stop calling you 'Virgie' you should sign your full name to all your school papers and letters. That's what I did when I wanted them to stop calling me 'Lizzie' and it worked." Why, yes, it did, Virgie thought. I haven't heard anyone say "Lizzie" for a long time. We all think of her as "Elizabeth" now.

Turning to David, she said apologetically, "I don't know anything different to do. What did they suggest?"

"Someone said you could write a paper on 'My Dream'."

"Oh, I wouldn't know how to do that."

"I think you can, Virg—Virginia," David replied confidently. Virgie glanced at him quickly to see if he seemed serious.

"I'll help you" assured David, "and I don't think it'll be so hard once you get started. You can think of things to put in while you're here at home and we'll talk about it when I come next week."

Virginia was able to return to school by the middle of the week. She found she was ahead of the class in most subjects, so this gave her extra time to work on her Literary paper. It had turned out to be fun once she realized that if she were writing about her dream she could include almost anything, no matter how imaginary.

Now as she sat in study hall and watched Queenie Shay and Maggie Peterson flirting with Mr. Mason, she got an idea. She jotted down, "In my dream I saw Mr. Mason no longer spending most of his time lingering at the desks of the older girls, but taking such a jolly interest in the younger ones." Would she dare to include that? She could just hear the titters when David read that part. Everyone knew Maggie and Queenie were vying for Mr. Mason's attention.

I can't understand what's happened to Maggie, Virginia

50

thought. Last year she and Dot and I had fun, but I guess even then she was kind of silly. She's the one who talked Pearl and me into reading Kate's letter. Now that we're in high school she seems so different. Or maybe I'm different. I'm enjoying my friendship with Lottie so much I guess the other girls think I don't want to be friendly with them. Lottie's invited me to her house on Sunday and Father said I could go.

Sunday was a beautiful winter day. Blue shadows lay on the snowbanks as Virgie and Lottie and her sister Mayme walked the quarter mile to Lottie's home. Bright sunlight hurt their eyes as it sparkled brilliantly on the glittering snow.

Virginia always enjoyed going to Lottie's house. It was so wonderful to be in a home where there was a mother, and here there was even a grandmother, as Lottie's Grandma Mellinger lived with them. And they had such a lovely farm. Virgie knew the Kellers had come to Butler County from Pennsylvania when Lottie was a baby. They had stayed right here and worked while Virginia's father had been trying to homestead in Kansas. So now the Kellers were buying their farm and Mike and Father were still renting.

Virginia didn't like to feel disloyal to Father, but she did enjoy visiting a farm that had such trim, snug, painted buildings—instead of the ramshackle ones on the hill farm.

Best of all, Lottie was such a good friend she never made Virgie conscious of her awkward, ill-fitting clothes the way some of the girls at school did. Virgie wished sewing wasn't so hard. Then maybe she and Pearl could make their own clothes instead of having the dressmaker in town make them large enough to last until they wore out.

Alice and John Streeter were at Kellers for dinner, too. Virginia kept glancing cautiously at John. He didn't look so different from other people, except for his mustache. Dunker men weren't supposed to wear mustaches, but many town men did, so that wasn't unusual. The Kellers all seemed to like him. He had twinkling blue eyes, and once he winked at Virginia when he caught her looking at him. She blushed and kept her eyes on her plate after that.

How can he not believe in God? she thought. Maybe he does, but he likes to keep people guessing—but he shouldn't tease about such an important thing.

Virginia couldn't believe her eyes when she and Lottie were putting dishes away in the pantry after Mrs. Keller's delicious meal. On the shelves sat sixteen pies—lemon, custard, pumpkin and nine with top crusts.

"Oh, my, what are all these?" Virgie breathed.

"Oh, Mother bakes twenty pies every Friday," Lottie replied casually.

"Like Mrs. Hassler, you mean? They say she's never served a meal without pie," Virginia commented.

"Oh, sometimes we run out, but Father doesn't like it when we do. He likes everything to be done just right. There, that's done. Let's go to my room," Lottie said, carefully putting away the cut glass cakestand.

The girls wandered through the house, stopping in the guest room to see the painted china wash bowl and pitcher Mrs. Keller had just gotten. On the bed rested Alice's new black bonnet, made of shiny material that tied with ribbons under the chin.

"Oh, did Alice get a new bonnet?" Virginia asked. "I thought you said she just got a new hat before Christmas."

"She did. But of course she can't wear it now."

"She can't? Why not?" Virgie asked in a puzzled tone. Lottie looked up from straightening the dresser scarf.

"Virginia May Wine! Don't tell me you've been going to church all these years and don't know that! She can't wear a hat now because she's joined the church. You know Dunker women always wear bonnets after they join the church. It's a sign, you know, of—of the change they've made," Lottie finished lamely, as if a little embarrassed to be speaking openly of such things.

"Oh, yes, of course, I forgot. But—but do they have to wear them?"

"Well, I guess so," Lottie replied decidedly. "You know

everybody does. And Sister Hersler said last Sunday that these things are very important! Come on. I want you to write in my new autograph album."

"Oh," Virginia said weakly, as she followed Lottie from the room. Somehow she had an uneasy, sinking feeling, but she couldn't quite think why.

The girls had a wonderful afternoon, giggling at the verses in the autograph album and sharing secrets. Pearl was a loyal sister, but a friend that she could tell everything to was a delightful new experience for Virginia.

"Goodness, Lottie, I wish you were still in school. The girls I used to be friends with all act so silly now. Since this is Pearl's last year, she's always busy studying for exams. Besides she's in a different class, so I don't see much of her. I only get to see you at church meetings."

In the evening David walked over to see Lottie's older brother Seth. Shortly after dark David and Virginia started home together. Virginia always looked forward to these walks with David, but tonight she didn't know what was the matter with her. She'd had a glorious afternoon, but way down deep something kept twisting and turning like a thorn caught in her clothing in the summer. It had something to do with the other girls at church. She kept remembering the way Flossie Hassler, Enid Miller and Sabetha Peters had looked when Virginia had started home with Lottie.

"A penny for your thoughts," teased David.

"I was thinking about the girls at church," Virginia said, soberly. "They didn't look very happy when I went home with Lottie today. I need someone to tell things to, so I tell them to Lottie. But what makes me feel bad is that the other girls are getting jealous because Lottie and I are together so much."

"Well now, it might be the girls need you more than Lottie does, and maybe you'd better divide up your attention," David replied.

"I don't know how I can do that. We're all together so there's not much time for secrets." I can't give up my friendship with Lottie when it means so much to me, Virginia thought. I suppose I could try to be friendlier to the girls at school and church, but no one understands me or makes me feel as comfortable as Lottie. Still I don't want to be uppity. Dot Burden has been asking me to come over and see her. Maybe I will go."

Chapter 8.
WAR STORIES

On a Saturday afternoon not too long after her visit with Lottie, Virginia walked to Shrevesville. She and Pearl had rushed through their work in the morning, so Pearl could study. Virginia had promised Dot Burden a visit.

There had been more snow during the week, but now it was thawing again. The road was soft and muddy, but when Virginia tried to walk on the snowbanks and stay out of the mud, the crust broke and she kept falling through to the soft snow beneath. Her stockings and skirts were wet, but it was such a beautiful day that she didn't mind. White puffs of clouds sailed in an infinite blue sky. The wind still had a bite in it and Virginia knew there would be more winter, but the promise of spring was in the late February air.

As she neared Shrevesville she met Dot's Grandpa McManus with his horse, Aleck, pulling the top buggy. The McManuses were Virginia's nearest neighbors. Grandpa had been blinded in the Civil War, but that never stopped him from going to town. There were three stops he made in Shrevesville. Aleck knew all of them and would go to each one in turn. If Grandpa didn't want out at the first stop, he'd start Aleck off again. When Grandpa was ready to go home, he'd get back in the buggy and lift the lines.

Now Virginia called, "Hello, Grandpa McManus" as she met the buggy. He lifted his buggy whip in reply.

"Oh, come in, Virgie—I mean Virginia," Dot said when Virginia knocked on her door. "What do you want to do?

55

We just got some new slides for our magic lantern, and I wanted to show you those, but my brother broke the lens the other day and we'll have to send to Omaha for another one. But first he has to earn the money for it from his job at the livery stable, so I don't know when we'll get to see them. I've been wanting you to write in my autograph book. You should see what Henry Nellman wrote!"

Oh, dear, I wish I hadn't come, thought Virginia, if she's going to talk about boys all the time. Henry hadn't paid any attention to Virginia since the May basket incident last spring and she didn't mind. He didn't look so interesting this year. He was always stumbling over his own feet and his voice kept falling from high to low. After examining each message in the book, and adding her own, Virginia and Dot discussed school.

"Are you going to enter something in the Omaha exposition?" asked Dot.

"Oh, I don't think so. I haven't heard very much about it," Virginia answered.

"Well, it would be a great honor to have something for people from all over the world to see, but I'd never attempt it. My writing looks like hen scratches and I can't draw at all. Would you like to look at our photograph album? It's a little too cold to sit in the parlor, but we'll bring it in here."

"All right."

In a moment Dot returned, carefully carrying the heavy book, its puffy plush cover stamped in gold leaf. Many of the pictures were wedding photographs or family groups, the men sitting stiffly on a stool, the women and children standing woodenly around them, all looking extremely serious. In the center of the book were several pictures of soldiers in various uniforms.

"These are mostly of my Grandpa McManus," Dot said.

"I saw him today as I walked in. I think it's wonderful the way Aleck knows just where your Grandpa wants to go," Virginia said politely, wishing she could change the subject.

56

"Here's a picture of Grandpa after the Battle of Antietam. That's where he got the most notches on his gun," Dot said proudly. "Did I ever tell you how many men Grandpa killed? You should see his gun! It's just *full* of notches! He really got rid of a lot of enemy soldiers before he lost his sight at Gettysburg."

"I think that's awful." Virginia stood up suddenly and Dot had to catch quickly at the sliding album. "My father was in the Civil War, too, and he wouldn't kill anyone, not even under orders! My father would *never* kill anyone!"

"Well, everyone to his own ideas," Dot sniffed. "I wouldn't think he'd be much good to the Army if he wouldn't kill. That's what he was there for."

"But he—he was a cook," Virginia stammered confusedly. "Look, Dot, I—I really must go on home now. It's getting late and—and I must help Pearl with the evening work. Thanks ever so much for inviting me. Your new autograph album is lovely. If I ever get one I'll be sure to ask you to write in it."

"Sure, Virgie, come again sometime," Dot said, but she didn't sound as if she meant it.

Virginia was glad to get out into the cold, clear air. The ground was starting to freeze, which made walking easier. The sun was setting, painting the western sky and clouds with many shades of pink, lavendar, orange and a clear, clear color—half yellow, half pale green—that Virginia couldn't name, but it looked as if it stretched clear into heaven.

She tried to drink in the beauty, but couldn't ignore the feelings clamoring within her. Well, David, I tried being friendly to someone besides Lottie, she thought, and it just made me lose my temper. I know Dot can't be expected to understand how Dunkers feel about killing, but how can *anyone* brag about how many men he's killed? Why don't people brag about how many wives' and sweethearts' hearts were broken? About how many children had to grow up without a father?

Virginia was still upset after supper. Mike and Father had come in from chores, and David was there until Sunday night. Father loved to pop corn and was busy at it now, since the long evening stretched ahead.

"What's the matter, McGinty?" Mike asked, using an old nickname. Virginia hated the name, but every so often Mike would remember it.

"Oh, I was visiting Dot Burden today and she started on her same old story of how many men Grandpa McManus killed in the War. I've heard it so many times and I just think it's awful. I—I lost my temper and told her so."

"Well, good for you!" exclaimed David.

" 'Good'! But, David, I was her guest! I was trying to be nice to her, the way you said I should, but I just couldn't stand to hear any more about how many men he killed at the Battle of Antietam."

"Maybe he didn't kill as many as he says," Pearl suggested. "Maybe he just wants to make a good story."

"Well, somebody did a lot of shooting," Father said soberly. "Antietam was called the bloodiest battle of the war. Did you know there was a Dunker church on the battlefield, and they took the wounded there?"

"No!" breathed Virginia. "Tell me about it."

"I dunno too much about it," Father admitted, emptying a skillet of hot corn into the dishpan on the table. "I guess there are bullets still stuck in the walls of the church. Some of my family stopped there when they went to Annual Meeting in Pennsylvania a few years ago. They said the sisters hadn't been able to scrub the blood stains out of the floor."

Virginia shuddered.

"But your family lived in Virginia. Wasn't the war a bad time for them? What did Brethren do when they couldn't fight because of their beliefs?" she asked. The corn rattled as Father dropped another handfull into the skillet.

"It was a bad time for everyone," he answered. "Many of us were opposed to slavery and to secession as well as to fighting, just like the Brethren in the north, but it was more unpopular for us than for them."

"Were there many slaves in your part of Virginia?" asked Pearl.

"Oh, yes. Many times we saw the soul drivers using whips on the slaves they had just bought as they drove them past our house." Father's voice broke and his eyes filled with tears. Virginia had never heard him mention slavery without tears.

The room was silent until David cleared his throat. "Tell us about your father," he requested.

"Grandpa? What about him?" Virginia asked.

"When he was accused of treason," Mike added.

"*Treason?*" Virginia dropped the handful of popcorn she was about to put in her mouth, and got down on the floor to pick it up. Father roused himself from his thoughts.

"My father was accused of treason when he fed some Union soldiers who had escaped from a Confederate prison. They were hidin' on the mountain back of our house, sick and almost starved. My father helped 'em instead of reporting 'em to the military authorities."

"In the Confederacy that would have been treason, all right," Pearl agreed.

"After they went on, Confederate soldiers came to take Father to Harrisonburg to stand trial," related Father.

"How did they know what he had done?" breathed Virginia, wide-eyed.

"We never found out who reported us, but there were plenty of people around who were jealous because we weren't goin' to the Army and were glad to get us in trouble."

"Well, what happened in Harrisonburg?" Pearl asked impatiently.

"Father admitted that he had fed and helped the Union soldiers. When they asked him if he didn't know it was death to do a thing like that in war time he said, 'Yes, I knew it.'

" 'And you deliberately disregarded the laws of your country and shielded its enemies?' asked the judge.

" 'No', Father said, 'I just regarded the laws of my Master, Jesus Christ, as havin' a higher claim on me than the laws of my country. He said, "If thine enemy hunger feed him, or do him good and pray for him" and that's what I done.' "

The room was silent except for the snappy sound of popping corn. Virginia's skin was crawling and her heart was beating so hard she thought she'd suffocate. Her own grandfather! How could anyone be so brave as to stand by his beliefs when he knew it might mean death?

David cleared his throat. "And then what happened?" he asked quietly. Father spoke with difficulty.

"I'll never forget what the judge said. I was sittin' in the back of the courtroom with my stepmother and sisters and Elder John Kline. I remember we all leaned forward to hear every word. The judge turned to the jury and said, 'No human law can be justified in condemning an action like that. It is a service he would render to any man, at any time or place at any cost. There was no intention to harm his country or help her enemy. It was a service born of allegiance to his Maker and will serve as effectively to overcome the enemy as any human force we can muster.' And he released Father to go home."

"Oh-h-h-h," Virginia sighed. She carefully set her popcorn bowl on the table with shaking hands.

After a moment Mike said, "Now tell us about you."

"Oh, I don't want to," Father murmured.

"I think you should, Father. The girls should know what Dunkers have done for their beliefs," David stated firmly.

"Well, I didn't do much. But maybe they should know. We had all worked hard and when the War began Father was fairly well off. I had five sisters and three brothers, all older. Most of them were married and lived close around. We all helped each other. When the war began my father paid for substitutes to enter the army instead of my brothers and my sisters' husbands."

"How did that work?" Virginia interrupted.

"Anyone who didn't want to go to the army could pay for someone else to go in his place," Father explained, emptying another skilletfull of fluffy white corn.

"But that wasn't fair!" Pearl cried indignantly.

"Some of the Dunkers didn't think we should do it, but my married brothers had young families and were needed at home. We were all opposed to slavery as well as killing. John Kline and the other church leaders tried hard to get the government to excuse us, but it was a very uncertain time. Every state had different laws and they kept changing.

"Some of the Brethren couldn't afford to pay for substitutes and Father paid for several not in our family. So when I was called, there wasn't any more money. I didn't know what else to do, so I went into the Confederate army as a cook. I was the youngest of the family and had always helped my stepmother in the house."

"So that's how you know so much about cooking and housekeeping," Virginia exclaimed in surprise.

"Shh-h-h-h. Go on, Father," Pearl urged impatiently.

"It looks like no one is eating pop corn, so I'd better quit." Father sat down and picked up the sock he was knitting. "I wasn't happy as a cook, because it was helpin' the army, but I didn't know what else to do. The war was going badly, and in '63 President Davis ordered all of us who weren't fightin' to go into the ranks. The Army was supposed to get Negroes to do our work."

"Oh, Father, what did you do?" Virginia cried. Father's hands were shaking.

"I run away one night. I hid in the daytime and run at night."

"But wasn't it dangerous?" Pearl asked.

"Of course it was," Mike answered. "They shot deserters on sight."

"Once I hid in a wheat field," Father continued. "This was very soon after I left and I knew they were lookin' for me. I could hear the soldiers callin' to each other as they hunted me. I didn't dare move, but I saw their horses' feet only a few rows away." Father's voice faded away.

"Oh, Father!" Virginia sobbed. Tears were running down her face and she didn't care. Her own good, kind father, who was so gentle and loving, being hunted like a criminal and all because he wouldn't kill another person!

"Did you go home?" asked Pearl.

"No. I knew they'd come there lookin' for me. I thought if I could get to Ohio I'd be safe. Many of our people had gone West to escape being drafted and I had a pretty fair idea of the way. I traveled in the woods and mountains. The Negroes I met told me how to go and which white people would help me. Once a girl guided me and some union soldiers through a bad stretch of mountains. The soldiers had been captured and escaped and were trying to get back to their lines."

"Did you get to Ohio safely? Did your family ever find out where you were?"

"When I got to Ohio I sent word back to my family. I made my way to a Dunker community and stayed there."

David stood up and stretched. "Thank you, Father, for telling us this again. It's good to remember what our forbears have been through."

"Oh, there are many others who suffered more and gave more for their convictions than I did," Father replied quickly. "My father's father moved to Virginia from Maryland at the end of the Revolutionary War because the gov'ment took his land."

"Why did they do that?" Virginia asked, puzzled.

"Because he wouldn't fight on either side, not for the English and not for the colonists," Father replied.

"Then he was a Dunker, too," Pearl stood beside the stove to warm up.

"Yes. Annual Meeting of 1794 was held in the upper room of his house. But I doubt if his household stayed up this late at night when meeting was the next day. We'd better get to bed." Father stretched and yawned.

Virginia lay awake a long time that night. She couldn't

get the stories Father had told out of her mind. Tears ran down her face unchecked as she thought again of the danger Father had been in. How lonely he must have been as he made his way West, never knowing if he would see his family again. I'm lonely with my family all around me! She thought. How much worse it must have been for Father!

Was this what it meant to be a Christian? Was this what God expected of people? Where did you get courage enough to stand up for what you believed, even when your life was in danger?

I'm such a shy little goose I could never do anything like that, but oh, God, I wish I could, Virginia prayed. I want to be good. I want to live the way You want me to, but I could never be as brave as my father and his father and grandfather. You'll just have to take me the way I am, because I can't do any better without Your help.

Chapter 9.
NOTES AND SIGNALS

"Father, I'll wager Virginia hasn't told you about her latest school honor," Pearl said one Monday evening in March as they sat at the supper table. Outside, the eaves were dripping and great patches of soft, black soil were exposed where the snow had disappeared under the warmth of the spring sun.

"Well, now, I don't wanta wager with you, but what is it? I know our little Virgie's right smart, but I dunno if I've heard about this or not," Father replied.

"You know the Omaha Exposition is being held this summer. The people planning it have sent word to all Nebraska schools asking for pupils' work to exhibit," Pearl began.

"Well, now, that's fine. I guess we'll show 'em that Nebraska schools can turn out good scholars," Father said with satisfaction.

"They especially mentioned maps, so Mr. Vining asked Charles Fettering and me to draw maps of the United States," Virginia continued. "We can look at a map as we work. And we're allowed to use a ruler to block out distances, but all the actual drawing has to be done freehand," explained Virginia. The big map we're following is ten years old, so it doesn't have the new states. Today I was following it so carefully I forgot all about Idaho, Washington, Montana and Wyoming! So tomorrow I have to correct that. Of course I couldn't forget Utah, since it's only about three

64

months old. I'm sure this map will never get to the 1896 Omaha Exposition!"

"I'm right proud of you, Virgie. Could you bring it home some night for me to see?" Father still called her "Virgie," though everyone else was trying hard to change.

"I don't know, Father. Mr. Vining is letting Charles and me work at a certain table in the political economy room, so we can leave everything out when we're not working. It would be hard to bring home, but of course you can see it when it comes back from Omaha. If it's good enough to go, that is," Virginia added hastily, as she rose to clear the table. Meanwhile, her thoughts began circling in a familiar groove.

Since the night a month ago when she listened to Father's Civil War stories, Virginia had been exploriing her new ideas about joining the church. She almost felt as if she and God had an agreement, but she realized this wasn't enough. The family had been attending revival meetings at the Baptist church and that evangelist put great importance on witnessing before men. He made it very plain that it wasn't enough just to promise God you'd be good. You had to stand up and be counted before everyone.

Virginia knew this was true, but she wanted to join the Dunker church, and they put great stress on "counting the cost." So she'd been trying to think what it would cost her to join the church. The thought of publicly drawing attention to herself by "going forward" or being baptized almost made her sick, but she was learning she could clench her fists and make herself do some things in spite of her shyness. Since she wasn't a man, she didn't have any bad habits to give up, such as chewing tobacco or swearing, but of course she had plenty to learn about being kinder and more loving.

Alice and John Streeter had attended every one of the meetings at the Baptist church. John even came to Sunday services with Alice quite often now. Everyone was amazed and said you never could tell.

When the kitchen was cleaned up, Pearl sat down to

study for examinations. Virginia knew she was hoping to go to Teachers' Institute in the summer, if they could find the money it would take. Virginia went to her room to write a note to Lottie. They had exchanged many notes during the winter, thanks to Lottie's younger brother, Edwin, who was their messenger.

Virginia chewed on her pencil and looked out the window. It was growing so dark she would soon have to light the lamp. Almost as if in answer to her thought a light suddenly appeared in Lottie's house, west down the ravine. Hurriedly, Virginia lit the kerosene lamp, adjusting the wick carefully so it would not smoke the glass chimney. Cleaning lamp chimneys was a job she did *not* like.

"Oh, Apple Blossom," she wrote," I have the jolliest idea! Just as I was thinking I must light the lamp I saw a light from your house. Why couldn't we signal each other during the day, too? We could agree on a certain day and time and each of us hang a sheet out the window. That would be our sign that we are remembering each other. What do you think?

Your ever loving
Goldenrod"

Next day the note was entrusted to Edwin and Lottie's answer was returned on Wednesday.

"My dearest Goldenrod,

How lucky I am to have such a clever girl for a friend. The sheet signals are a capital idea! How about tomorrow at five? We'll both be home then and can probably sneak away to wave to one another. I can hardly wait. It'll be such fun!

"I have to go now, as Mother is ill with the grippe and I haven't much time. Let me know if tomorrow at five is a good time.

Love,
Your Apple Blossom"

During lunch hour Virginia took a few moments to reply that Lottie's suggestion was all right. Not many friends can signal to each other from their own windows, she thought, as she searched the playground for Edwin.

After school Virginia hurried up the muddy street to the post office, enjoying the fresh spring air after the stuffy schoolroom. The playful wind tugged at her brown hair, which was pulled back severely from the widow's peak on her high, wide forehead. Her dress was growing short again, and it made her feel awkward, but she knew they couldn't think of spending money on a school dress so near the end of the year.

There was no one at the post office but Sister Miller, Virginia's Sunday School teacher. Mrs. Paineson, the postmaster's wife, was showing her the latest copy of *Godey's Lady's Book*. They looked up as Virginia came in.

"Hello, Virginia," Mrs. Miller said in a friendly manner. "Would you like to see the latest styles? It's a good thing I don't live in the East. I know my clothes would never pass muster!"

"No, thank you, I really don't have time. I just came to get the mail," Virginia replied. She liked Mrs. Miller, but felt shy around Mrs. Paineson, a large woman with a few black hairs growing on her chin.

"There's a letter here for your father. Looks like it's from his kinfolk in Virginia," Mrs. Paineson said loudly, holding the letter to the light.

It's none of your business who it's from, Virginia thought angrily, but she thanked Mrs. Paineson and left with Sister Miller.

"It's interesting to look at the latest fashions, Virginia, but just think how much good all that money could do on the mission field. You know our church just began mission work in India last year. In a recent *Gospel Messenger* there was a letter from Brother Stover, telling of the great need there. I must remember to bring it for the mission report in class on Sunday."

"Yes, Sister Miller. You have a very pretty bonnet."

"Thank you, dear. Grey is all right for town, but of course I'd wear only black to church. Good bye now. I'll see you on Sunday."

"Good bye." Virginia hurried along the muddy street, but suddenly she stopped short, feeling as if a bolt of lightning had struck her. What had Sister Miller said? "A grey bonnet is all right for town, but I'd wear only black to church." A bonnet! I don't have a bonnet of any color, Virginia thought. Pearl and I are too young to wear hats, and Elizabeth is such a tomboy she always goes bareheaded. I can't join the church without a bonnet, but I haven't any money. I've been trying to count the cost of joining the Brethren church, but I never thought about clothes.

Reaching home at last, Virginia hurried down the lane and into the house. On the table was a pan of peeled potatoes soaking in cold water. A platter of sliced ham was covered by a big lid. Dear, dear Father, Virginia thought. How kind and thoughtful he always is. He must have done this when he came in at noon.

All during the evening part of her mind stayed on her new problem. Where in the world could she get the money to buy a bonnet so she could join the church? It wasn't the kind of problem she could share with just anyone. A man wouldn't understand how embarrassing it would be to be baptized and then not have a bonnet for the next Sunday.

What had Lottie said when they were discussing Alice's bonnet? "Dunker women wear bonnets as an outward sign of the change they've made when they join the church, and Sister Hersler says it's very important." Brother Hersler was the main preacher in their church, so certainly Sister Hersler would know.

Yes, she just had to have a bonnet, but Father certainly didn't have the money for such a thing, even if she could bring herself to ask him. If she mentioned what she wanted, she'd have to say that she was thinking of joining the church, and she wasn't quite ready to do that yet, even though she'd have to sometime.

As she finished the dishes Virginia realized she didn't

even know how much money she needed. Maybe it wasn't as bad as she feared. Before she went to bed, Virginia wrote a note to Lottie.

"Dear Apple Blossom, I can hardly wait till tomorrow at five. It'll be such fun! Be sure you don't forget!

"When I was at the post office today, Mrs. Paineson was showing Sister Miller the latest *Godey's Lady's Book*. You should see some of those hats! Flowers, fruit and feathers! It's really worldly! I think our little Dunker bonnets are so much better. By the way, do you know what Alice's black bonnet cost? It's so pretty and silky. Don't forget tomorrow!

> Yours,
> Goldenrod"

Thursday dawned bright and clear. Virginia gave the note to Edwin and tried to concentrate on studying. It would be fun to signal with the sheets and tomorrow she'd get an answer back about the cost of Alice's bonnet. Until then she'd try not to worry. Working on the map took all her concentration. Whenever she thought about something else she made mistakes.

That night Virginia hurried home. She didn't quite want to tell Pearl what she and Lottie were doing. Pearl was usually pretty understanding, but she was two years older and she might think this was too childish.

At almost five o'clock, Virginia slipped away to her room. Carefully unfolding a clean sheet, she hung it out the window, shivering in the brisk air. Yes, in a few minutes there was a white square hanging below Lottie's window, showing white above the dark porch roof underneath.

What fun! Virginia thought. She didn't forget, after all. Look, she's shaking her sheet. I'd better shake mine, so she'll know I'm here. But why is she shaking it again? And again? My arms are getting tired. It's hard to lean out the window and keep shaking like this. Is she making fun of me? That's not like Lottie. Well, I've got to get back to the

69

kitchen. I'll just leave mine hanging here so she can see it. We'll do this again sometime. It's fun!

Before school next morning, Edwin sidled up to Virginia. "Here's a note from Lottie."

Virginia opened the letter and read:

"My dearest Goldenrod,
   Whatever happened to you this afternoon? I hope nothing is wrong at your house to make you forget our plan. Why didn't you shake your sheet? I shook mine so many times I got tired, but I never did see yours.
   Alice's bonnet cost $1.75. She said there were some there for a dollar, but they weren't very good.
   How is the map coming?
   I'm still so disappointed that you forgot about our signaling, but I hope nothing serious has happened.
                                        Yours,
                                        Appleblossom"

Virginia stood stock still, trying to make sense of it. Forgot? Of course I didn't forget. I was there shaking it just like she was and I left it hanging when I went back to the kitchen. How can she say she didn't see it?

One dollar and seventy-five cents! That's a terrible amount of money. Even a dollar is more than I could ever get. Elizabeth has to work out for a whole week just for a dollar and a half! I didn't dream bonnets were so expensive. Whatever will I do? Well, the bell's ringing, so I guess I'd better go in to school for now.

At noon, Virginia wrote back.

"Dear Apple Blossom,
   What do you mean, you couldn't see my sheet? I thought you were shaking yours just to mock the way I shook mine. Surely you could see it. It was such a sunny day.
   Oh, Apple Blossom, do you think that was the reason? I've noticed that our house looks a lot whiter

70

when the sun is shining on it than it really is. Maybe the sheet didn't show up against the light siding. I'm so sorry you were disappointed, but I really didn't forget. Let's try it again at a different time of day and use something dark.

The map is coming all right, I guess, but I wish I could hurry and get done with it. Today Mr. Vining said my mountain range marks were too big. I guess I'm getting too impatient.

See you in two days, my darling Apple Blossom. Please forgive me about the sheet.

Your Goldenrod"

Virginia knew why her map hadn't gone well that day. She just couldn't stop thinking about that dollar! That was so much money! A dollar would buy three large sacks of groceries or enough material for several dresses. The most she had ever had was twenty-three pennies, and once Pearl had saved forty-seven cents. But where in the world would she ever get a dollar? Surely, surely there must be a way, but what was it?

Chapter 10.
THE NEST IN THE CORNCRIB

"Ouch! Oh, biddy, I'm not going to hurt you. Just let me have that egg!"

Virginia rubbed the angry red mark on her arm where the broody hen had pecked viciously. She hated to gather eggs this time of year. Father had set most of the hens a week ago, but some of the rest were still broody. They sat on their nests in the chicken house, clucking angrily and pecking hard when Virginia tried to take the egg they'd laid that day.

Father could do it so well. Talking quietly to the hen, he deftly wrapped a burlap sack around her head so she couldn't peck, at the same time reaching quickly but gently beneath her soft, warm feathers to take the egg she was defending. Virginia had watched him dozens of times, but she could never get the burlap around the hen's head in just the right way. Usually it was too loose, and her hands were underneath it so the hen had plenty of opportunity to peck while Virginia was feeling beneath her. It was amazing how fast that feathered neck could lash out when the hen wanted to protect her egg.

Now Virginia stood rubbing her arm and trying to decide what to do. Pearl would take a stick and poke at the hen, prying her up till she finally jumped off the nest and ran into the chicken yard, protesting loudly at such treatment. Virginia hated to do that, but she feared that sharp beak more.

"Well, I'll just leave you alone," she muttered, "While I feed the setting hens. If you decide to get down to eat I can get the egg then."

Virginia opened the gate in the makeshift partition across one end of the chicken house. Quietly she went from one cage to another, lifting the slats so the hens could get out to eat and drink. The hens must not be excited or they would leave the nest too long, and once the eggs grew cold they wouldn't hatch. Virginia filled the food and water pans, then slipped back through the gate. The broody hen was still on the nest, glaring at Virginia with beady eyes.

"Poor old biddy. You want to be a mother, too, don't you? Father's already set all the hens for this year, so you'll just have to lay eggs for us to eat."

But why? Virginia thought suddenly. Why not set this one? Father said we had enough hens setting, so he surely wouldn't mind if I set this one myself. I could raise the chicks and sell them to people in town to get money for my bonnet. If I fed the chickens till they were real fat, I could maybe get fifteen cents a piece for them.

Virginia stood perfectly still, thinking about this new idea. She'd want the project to be a secret, so she would need a safe place to hide the hen. Could she get enough eggs? Eggs were scarce while the hens were setting. Would it be deceitful to take from the table supply? Mike might laugh at her, and Father would feel bad that he didn't have a dollar to give her. Pearl was already disappointed that there wasn't money for her to attend Teachers' Institute this summer.

Shivering, Virginia lingered in the chilly April afternoon. She really should go and help Pearl with supper, but she needed to get the hen settled, too. Behind the granary was an old corncrib which Mike had said should be torn down, as he thought it was a good place for rats. No one ever goes there, Virginia thought. I could fix a nest and put the hen there.

Finding an old crate, she partially filled it with straw and carried it to the dirty, ramshackle corncrib, trying not to think about rats. Then she went to the kitchen and looked in the egg crock. She had gotten eight eggs tonight, which were still in the chicken house. There was one under the hen, so if she took three from the house, that would make a dozen. Pearl would wonder where today's eggs were, so maybe she shouldn't set so many, but a couple probably wouldn't hatch and a couple might die. She'd need a whole dozen if she were going to have enough grown chickens.

The kitchen had been empty when Virginia entered, but now she heard Pearl coming down the stairs. Quickly she snatched up three eggs and hurried out. She hadn't felt this guilty since she and Pearl read Katie's letter. How long ago that seemed! She stopped in the chicken house to get the day's eggs. "Just a minute, biddy. I've got big plans for you," she said to the hen, who was still watching her suspiciously.

Virginia arranged the eggs carefully in the straw nest beneath the crate, wondering how one hen could stretch enough to cover a dozen eggs. She'd come every day with food and water and in three weeks the chicks would hatch.

Now came the hard part. An old jacket of Mike's was hanging inside the granary door. Virginia took it down and held it carefully away from her, thinking of spiders. Inside the chicken house, she crept quietly up to the broody hen. Suddenly Virginia dropped the coat around the hen and quickly picked her up, reaching for the egg beneath.

Forgetting the spiders, she tucked the struggling, squawking hen beneath her arm and hurried to the corncrib. Just as she reached the granary the hen, pecking and clawing beneath the coat, gave a lurch. Virginia grabbed for her, and in doing so squeezed too tightly the warm egg she held in her hand. She could feel its gooey contents dropping onto her stocking.

"Oh, bother," Virginia said, as she reached the corncrib. She thrust the hen as gently as she could beneath the crate, at the same time trying to clean her hand on some straw. To her relief, the hen began pushing the eggs around with beak and feet until they were adjusted satisfactorily, then nestled down on them with a satisfied cluck.

"All right, biddy, now we're both happy. You've only got eleven eggs, but we'll just have to make those do. I'll be out every day with food and water. You do your part and I might get that bonnet yet."

Pearl didn't seem to notice the missing eggs. Every day Virginia fed and watered the hen when she did the other chicken chores. She still felt a little guilty for not asking Father's permission, but it was for *such* a good cause. Surely it couldn't be too bad. And after the weekend it seemed more urgent than ever.

Chapter 11.
BAPTISM

David was home the next Sunday. After dinner he said, "Virginia, how about taking a walk with me?"

"All right, David. I'd like to. Why don't we go up into the pasture? I want to see if the bluebells are blooming yet. I love them so."

The April sun was warm, but the wind was cool. The clear air stretched away for miles, and as they climbed the ridge above the house the whole world seemed alive with spring.

"I guess it's a little too early for bluebells," Virginia said. "They're one of the things I like best about this farm."

"Aren't the prairie dogs your favorites, too?" teased David, as he gestured to the prairie dog "town."

"They're fun to watch, but I don't like to get too close because of the rattle snakes," Virginia replied.

"We only have small towns this far East," David said. "Farther out in the state they have towns that cover as much as ten acres, I've heard."

"Look, there are some. Let's sit here out of the wind and watch them," Virginia suggested. "If we stay this far away they won't go into their holes."

"And no snakes will sneak up behind us," David grinned.

Virginia made a face at him and settled herself on the side of the hill. Below them the ground was bare where the prairie dogs had eaten away the grass. Little mounds

marked the entrance to each hole. Many of the dogs, looking like ground squirrels, were sitting upright on their
mounds, surveying the area around. Others were running
around busily. The wind prevented Virginia from hearing
the chirping, whistling sounds she knew they were making,
but suddenly they heard a sharp bark from the sentinel the
prairie dogs had posted. At once all of them disappeared
into their holes and the entire town lay silent and deserted,
with only the April wind left alive.

"He must have thought he heard a coyote," David said
lazily, twisting into a more comfortable position.

It was pleasant sitting in the warm sun. Virginia could
almost forget her guilt at deceiving Father about the hen
and eggs. The hen was going to be a good mother. Surely
the chickens would all grow up. There must be some people
in town who didn't keep their own chickens and would be
glad to buy some next fall. If I can just keep from being too
impatient, Virginia thought, I can get the money to buy my
bonnet. Then I can join the church.

"Virginia, I want to tell you something." David interrupted her thoughts. "I'm going to be baptized next Sunday. I'd like you to be at the service."

Virginia's heart stopped. What kind of joke is this? she
thought. I'm the one that wants to be baptized, so why
should David . . .? But why not? He has as much right to
join the church as anyone. It's his responsibility too,
though he's already so good I don't see how he could be better. She realized David was watching her curiously. She
had to say something, but how could she when she was
suffocating?

"That—that's wonderful, David. I'm—I'm so glad for
you," she said faintly.

"I've been thinking about it for some time. Those meetings at our church last winter really got me started. And listen to this. I was over to see Alice and John Streeter last
night. John will be baptized, too."

"Oh, David, really? Are you sure?"

"Yes. You know he's been coming to church a lot since Alice joined. He's really a thinker. We've been having some good talks."

"But—but why did everyone always say he was an infidel? I—I don't understand," Virginia stammered.

"I don't know why they said that, but it just shows we shouldn't label people. John has a little more education than some people and thinks a little differently than they do. Maybe he's been more honest in his search for God than some of those who criticized him, but I shouldn't judge them either. Anyway, he's coming into the church and we must be sure to welcome him."

"Oh, of course. I'm sure the Kellers must all be happy."

Virginia couldn't remember afterward how they got back from the pasture or what they talked about. There was such a mixture of feelings within her! She was glad for David, but somehow she'd thought she'd be the first of the family to join the church. Surely she didn't have to wait till last just because she was the youngest! It wasn't wrong of her to want a dollar so she could get a bonnet, was it? Of course if she were a boy she wouldn't have this problem, but she mustn't be jealous. Mike, David and Father worked hard so she could stay in school. It wasn't their fault that crops had been poor and prices were low.

By the middle of the week Virginia had decided that this was a test of her determination and she'd just have to be patient. Surely everything would work out at the right time. She was delighted that the hen was setting so well.

But on Thursday as Virginia and Pearl reached the top of the ridge above the farm, they heard Buster barking furiously.

"Whatever is the matter with Buster?" Pearl asked. "He doesn't usually bark like that."

Running into the yard, the girls found Buster rolling on the grass, shaking himself and whining piteously, reeking of skunk odor. Her heart in her mouth, Virginia ran to the corncrib, where mute evidence of tragedy lay scattered about. Buster had finished the skunk, but not before it had killed the trapped hen and broken the eggs.

Her eyes blinded with tears, and gagging from the terrible smell, Virginia removed the food and water pans and put the crate back where she'd gotten it. Mike would bury the skunk and the hen. She hoped he'd think the hen had stolen her nest. The broken eggs lay messily in the straw. If it weren't for me, Virginia thought, we could have eaten those eggs and the hen would still be alive and pecking me. She started to laugh, but it turned into a sob. She must be a very bad girl to be so deceitful. Was this punishment for trying to get the money she needed?

"Virginia," Pearl called, "you ought to change your clothes or you'll get skunk odor on them. Why do you want to look at an old dead skunk anyway? And why are you crying?"

"Well, that smell is awful strong, you know," Virginia replied irritably. I can't do anything right, she thought angrily. All anyone does around here is criticize. But that isn't fair, either. They'd help me if they could. I've got to be happy this weekend for David's sake, but how can I when I'm so miserable inside?

The next day brought a letter that Katie had a chance to come home for a short visit. George couldn't come, but Katie and little Frank would be coming on Saturday afternoon. She was so eager to show the baby to her family.

The girls rushed home from school on Friday and worked far into the evening, getting up early Saturday morning to continue. Pearl was pale with fatigue by noon, but Virginia worked grimly on. It was a relief to have so much to do. Working so hard could make her forget all the questions she couldn't answer and the feelings she couldn't understand.

By the time Mike got back from Schuyler with Katie and the baby, the house was spotless, pies were cooling, supper was cooking and Pearl was looking better after her nap. It was so *wonderful* to have Katie back again and baby Frank was so cunning. Virginia wasn't used to babies, but something tight inside her eased a little when Frank clutched her finger in one fat little hand and looked at her with his huge blue eyes.

79

Elizabeth and David came home for the weekend to see Katie, so the family was together again for the evening— the first time since Katie's wedding day. They were all so happy and Virginia was able to tell herself that it was all right about tomorrow. Things would work out for her when it was her turn. In the meantime, she mustn't spoil their joy with her problems.

The next day after church, they all drove to the Platte. It was a hot day for early May and Katie had decided it would be all right to take little Frank, though she'd keep him at the wagon and not join the congregation.

When Mike had tied the horses, Virginia climbed down from the wagon, careful to keep her skirt away from the wheel. As she turned to look up at her sisters, her usually pale, sensitive face was flushed with the heat and her blue eyes seemed larger than ever beneath her high, wide forehead.

"Aren't you coming?" she asked.

"No, I guess not," said Elizabeth.

"We'll stay with Katie," Pearl explained. For a minute Virginia thought of doing the same. It would be easier. But, no, she couldn't do that to David. He'd been too good to her. And he'd especially asked her to come today.

Virginia turned and started to walk toward the people gathered beside the river bank for the baptismal service. As she stooped to tie her shoe, her sisters' voices came to her on the wind.

"It's hard to believe our shy little Virgie's almost fifteen. Has it really been twelve years since Mother died? So much has happened," said Elizabeth, tossing her windblown hair.

"I know, but the best part is that Father was able to keep us all together, just as Mother hoped," replied Katie. "And I don't believe Virgie's quite as shy as she used to be."

Virginia sighed. I may not be as shy, but I'm going to be fifteen next week and I'm still too dumb to figure out a way to get a bonnet, she thought as she walked on.

At the edge of the crowd she hesitated, all the mixed-up feelings coming back. It was so hot that even the river

80

didn't cool the ceaseless Nebraska wind, which was whipping the long skirts of the women. The Platte flowed sluggishly before them, its shallow mud flats marked by straggly cottonwood and willow trees, clothed in the new green of spring. A flock of crows wheeled and circled against the deep blue sky.

Brother Miller started another hymn, "To the Flowing Stream of Jordan." The congregation joined in, but their voices sounded thin and wavering, not strong and sure the way they did in church. Just then Lottie turned and beckoned.

Virginia moved quickly to her and both girls watched soberly as the applicants for baptism waded into the water and knelt before Brother Hersler. There were several others besides John and David. Virginia heard soft weeping when it was John's turn. People still were stunned by this evidence of God working in their midst.

She clenched her fists against the emotion swirling within her when it was David's turn. The wavering strains of the hymn, the cawing of the crows, and Brother Hersler's phrases—"In the name of the Father . . . and of the Son . . ."—echoed her confusion. Oh, David, my big, strong brother. Why can't I be as brave as you? Why can't I . . .?

Virginia's thoughts were interrupted as she realized that David was returning, a strange light on his face. She'd never seen him more radiant. Impulsively, she stepped forward, her short, slim figure erect, as he came up the bank. His damp arms went around her as he kissed her and whispered, "When are you coming, Sis?"

Oh, I want to, David, her heart cried silently. I want to so much, but—She smiled faintly at him and returned to Lottie's side, flushing as she realized that everyone had seen.

"Can't you come home with me, Virginia?" Lottie asked, when the service was over.

"Thanks for inviting me, Lottie, but I guess I'll go along home this time. You know Katie's here with the baby, and I want to be with them as much as possible," Virginia re-

81

plied, but she didn't really know what she wanted. She felt like running away to hide, but if she were alone she'd feel too lonely and confused. She'd never forgive herself if she spoiled the family's happiness. How could she pretend when she felt so miserable? It wasn't fair for David to join the church when she wanted to so much.

Oh, why couldn't she stop thinking? Or why couldn't she be a little girl again? Wasn't there any way she could stop all this misery inside her?

Chapter 12.
WATERMELONS

The map was finished and sent off to Omaha, but Virginia felt no joy in it. She was sure it was terrible and wouldn't even be hung. Her birthday came and went and the school term ended. Virginia watched Pearl receive her high-school diploma and wondered how she could be so calm over her disappointment about not going to Teachers' Institute. They talked about it one warm, windy day while they were washing and airing blankets and bed covers to be put away 'till fall.

"Pearl, I'm so sorry that your plans aren't working out for Teachers' Institute this summer. I just wish I had the money to give you. You've always been so good to me," Virginia declared as she struggled to hold a flapping blanket on the line. "The reason we've never fussed is that you always give in to me, and I don't deserve it. I've been plenty naughty to you sometimes. Remember how I used to pinch you when things weren't going my way?"

Pearl laughed. "That was because I could twist my nose around and you couldn't. That used to make you so angry."

"Yes, and you used to tease me by saying 'squash' because you heard me say that I thought it was an ugly word. I never could think of anything bad enough to say in return until I heard the word 'oak.' I thought that was almost as ugly as 'squash'!" Virginia laughed, then became sober again.

"What do you plan to do, Pearl, since you can't go to

83

school?" Virginia hated to say the words. They made it sound so final and reminded her that there was no money for her bonnet, either. She and Pearl started back to the house.

"Well, I'll just stay at home this summer, I guess. Goodness knows there's enough to be done around here. I haven't said too much to Father, because I'm sure he feels badly that I can't go to Institute, but maybe I can "work out" during harvest. If I'm able to do a good job, maybe I could "work out" for someone next winter and save enough money to go to school next summer."

"You're going to keep on trying then?" Virginia's shoulders ached from lifting the heavy comforts.

"Why, yes," Pearl said spiritedly. "I think that's what we're supposed to do. We just can't give up because things don't go our way the first time."

The girls were silent for a minute, then Virginia announced, "Pearl, if you'll help me carry out this basket before it leaks all over the floor, I'll hang these up. There ought to be a better way of wringing water out of clothes than just twisting them in your hands. I can never get them dry and the floor's always a mess."

"You should try stirring them with a rolling pin," Pearl laughed and Virginia joined her at this reference to an old family story.

When Father and Mother had come out to Nebraska twenty years before, the new settlers had been struggling to pay for their farms and hadn't many conveniences. Mother, straight from a prosperous Virginia home, had been shocked to see the neighbors stirring cornmeal mush with the rolling pin. It had been a family joke ever since.

When Pearl left her at the line Virginia's thoughts returned to the problem of her bonnet. She'd been wondering if the skunk's destroying the nest was God's way of punishing her for being deceitful. Or maybe she wasn't supposed to join the church now at all, but she couldn't believe God didn't want her. Surely it wasn't vain of her to want a bon-

84

net. All Dunker women wore bonnets! She just *couldn't* join the church without one!

Pearl says we should keep trying, Virginia thought. Maybe God is testing me to see how sincere I really am. Father doesn't have the money even if I asked him. So it's up to me. But how can I earn a dollar? I can't work out when I'm needed here at home and I can't think of any other way to earn money. Still, there must be something!

After dinner Virginia decided to clean the pantry. Back in a dark corner she found a jar of flat black seeds. "Pearl, what are these?" she called.

Pearl, mopping the kitchen floor, straightened up and leaned on the mop handle. "I wonder if they're seeds from that watermelon Mike thought was so good. Remember the one he brought home from David City last summer? The garden's all planted now. Why don't you just throw them out?"

Virginia stood still, the jar in her hand. Father didn't plant these, she thought, but I don't see why I can't. Then I could sell enough to get my dollar! Isn't this something! Just when Pearl convinces me I should keep trying I find these seeds! Surely I'm not being deceitful this time.

After supper Virginia restlessly walked about the farmyard. Where could she plant watermelon seeds? And suddenly, as she stood on the side of the draw beside the house, she knew. Near the bottom of the ravine was a level, sandy stretch. That would be perfect, Virginia thought. It would get plenty of sun and be sheltered from the wind. As long as there's water in the draw I could easily get water to the plants. And probably no one would notice them down there.

Slipping back to the house, she took the jar of seeds from the pantry shelf and returned to the draw. She wasn't sure how far apart they should be planted, but she poked holes in the sand with a stick and dropped the seeds in, covering them carefully as she'd seen Father do so many times.

Twilight had settled when she clambered back up the

85

side of the draw. The swallows were leaving their nests in the barn to fly out for insects. The sky was still light in the west, with a few rosy clouds high in the sky.

For the first time in weeks Virginia felt happy and relaxed. School was out, the summer was ahead and she'd found a way to earn the money for her bonnet. Surely everything would work out this time!

Every day Virginia found a few minutes to sneak down to the draw to check on the melons. It seemed they would never come up. What if the seeds were too old? Maybe they had been on the pantry shelf for years instead of just a few months!

But one morning flat, round leaves were poking through the ground. Virginia knelt above them, marveling at the miracle of seeds. She'd take such good care of them! They'd surely be the best and largest watermelons ever and maybe there'd be enough money left over from the bonnet for a new ribbon for her school shirtwaist.

When she went to church on Sunday, Virginia was almost tempted to tell Lottie, but she didn't. The Kellers had a prosperous farm, and even with Lottie it was embarrassing to say there wasn't an extra dollar to buy a bonnet.

Virginia watched David as he led the Sunday School devotions. He read the Bible in a strong voice as if it were interesting. He had been chosen Superintendent and everyone said what a fine job he was doing and that he was going to be a great church leader. David seemed so happy since he'd joined the church, as if he'd found something he'd been hunting a long time.

Virginia went home with Lottie after church. They planned to try signaling again, but this time they would use dark shawls. Virginia pointed out how light her house looked in the sunshine and they agreed that was why Lottie hadn't seen the sheet.

As Virginia walked home in the hot June twilight, heat lightning played along the horizon. Black clouds piled up in the sky and distant thunder rumbled. She arrived home to find Mike scanning the clouds anxiously. "What's the matter, Mike?" she asked.

"Father doesn't like the look of those clouds, and I don't either," Mike replied seriously. "Hail would ruin the corn, and a hard rain would wash it out. I'd sure hate to have to replant it."

"But I thought we were always glad for rain," Virginia said. "It is awful when everything dries up in front of our eyes."

"That's true, but too much rain is too much. It'd solve a lot of problems if there were just some way to store it up and use it when we need it," Mike sighed.

Well, I don't know how we can control the weather, Virginia thought. She'd had such a happy day that she couldn't believe anything could spoil it.

When she woke before dawn, though, Virginia heard water rushing through the draw. Usually it made her feel cozy, but this was a dreadful sound. As soon as it was light, she dressed and rushed out, heedless of the clammy mud that clung to her bare feet and slowed her frightened steps.

Standing on the edge of the draw, Virginia could see that the water was much higher than the sandy flat where the young plants had grown so bravely. Her face wet with tears and raindrops, she turned heartbrokenly away. She found Mike standing on the doorstep, a discouraged slump to his shoulders.

"Well, it didn't hail, but it was a real gully-washer, all right. I hate to think how much corn I'll have to replant. And it's almost July. It'll probably dry up too soon for this second planting to make anything. But what are you doing out here, McGinty?" Needing to share her disappointment, Virginia ignored the disliked nickname.

"Oh, Mike, it washed away my watermelons!"

"What watermelons? It didn't get high enough to flood the garden."

"But *I* planted some down beside the draw where I could water them. And now they're gone and I can't . . ." She stopped, her secret almost out. Mike reached for his straw hat, hanging on a nail beside the door, and shook the water off it.

"You planted watermelons in the draw? What'd you do a silly thing like that for? You might know it'd flood and, besides, that soil is too sandy to grow anything but cockleburrs."

"Oh, Mike, don't say that," Virginia implored, her voice breaking. Mike shrugged, his honest face amazed.

"Well, I didn't mean to make you feel bad." He picked up the milkpail and stepped into the mud.

Virginia went miserably into the house to start breakfast. I'm so dumb I don't even know where to plant melons, she thought. He'd really laugh if he knew I was trying to earn a dollar. But now what? Where do I turn now? I thought I should keep trying, like Pearl said, but how can I when I don't know what to try next?

Chapter 13.
DAVID

July passed in a fog of questions and hard work. Pearl and Virginia both grew thin from working long hours in the garden, in the house, and preparing constant meals for the hungry men.

Virginia was glad for the work, though. If she worked hard enough she could forget for awhile the questions that plagued her. Where could she get the money for a bonnet? What was God trying to tell her? Why did everything she tried fail? Didn't God know or care how she felt? Surely if she could just join the church she wouldn't feel so lonely, so left out of things. Her mind seemed to wear a weary groove, asking the same questions over and over.

Even the beauty of a Nebraska summer couldn't reach her. In addition to the graceful swallows, Virginia had always loved the cheery song of the meadow lark. She and Pearl had often laughed about his musical command, "Fill up your *tea* kettle," but now the repetitious call almost made her angry.

The green and white blossom of Snow-on-the-mountain in the pasture and the lovely, lacy golden rod just beginning to bloom were unnoticed. Virginia had been delighted the year before when the legislature had chosen golden rod as the state flower, but now it didn't matter.

Mr. Vining stopped her on the street in Shrevesville to tell her he had been to the Exposition in Omaha and her map was indeed hanging in the school exhibit, though it hadn't won a prize. Virginia couldn't believe that only last winter it had seemed so important. Now she felt old and dull and tired. Literary and Musical Union meetings stopped during the summer as everyone was so busy in the fields, so there was no place to go but church, and church was almost worse than working.

David was working hard, too, and seldom got home, so Virginia saw him only at church. He was so capable and seemed so much at home doing church work. She was proud of him, but he seemed like a stranger and she was on the outside. Worse than her feeling about David, however, was trying to avoid John Streeter.

John was certainly a changed man. His new faith meant so much to him that he wanted to share it with everyone. He had made a list of the young people he was trying to convert and Virginia knew she was high on the list. He was so friendly and sincere and meant so well that Virginia couldn't be rude to him, but she dreaded to see him coming her way. He was David's friend and Lottie's brother-in-law but he was always so concerned about her soul and it only reminded Virginia of the turmoil she couldn't forget.

On a Sunday early in August she saw John coming toward her through the congregation. "Virginia, I want to ask you something. I want you to read the sixty-third Psalm every day for a week."

"All right, John. I guess I can do that." Surely reading the Bible wouldn't hurt her.

That night Virginia took down the Bible from the shelf where Father kept it and turned to the Psalm: "O God, thou art my God; early will I seek thee: my soul thirsteth for thee, my flesh longeth for thee in a dry and thirsty land, where no water is."

Well, it really wasn't God she longed for. She'd had kind of an understanding with God ever since last winter some time. It was the church fellowship she wanted to be a part of. Maybe she should join the Baptist church in town. She had school friends there and she'd been invited to join during their revival meetings. Baptist women didn't have to wear bonnets, so there'd be no problem of money. But she wanted to be Brethren, like her ancestors before her. Somehow she'd feel disloyal to the courage of her father and grandfather if she joined another church. But, then, why didn't God help her find a way to earn the money?

Every day Virginia read the Psalm, because she'd promised, but each reading made her feel worse. By Sunday she thought she'd explode if anyone so much as looked at her. As soon as church was over, she fled to the wagon, hoping no one would come looking for her. Her heart sank when David came out with the family, explaining that he had the rest of the day off. She was so miserable she didn't even want David around.

He seemed to pay no attention to her, however, and chatted with Pearl about who had been at church. Virginia busied herself with dinner and in the afternoon David, Mike and Father walked out to the fields and looked at the crops. Mike's second planting of corn was doing fairly well, but rain was really needed.

Virginia was restless all afternoon and was glad when it was finally time for her chicken chores. But there in the chicken house she remembered the day she'd set the hen and all that had happened since. It's no use, she thought. I can't earn a dollar, so I can't get a bonnet, so I can't join the church. It's just hopeless. There isn't any way out.

Shaking the quick tears away impatiently, she carried the basket of eggs to the house, where supper was waiting. The family seemed subdued and quiet as they ate. Afterward they scattered to finish the evening chores. Virginia thought David had returned to the farm where he worked, but when she finished the dishes he was standing in the doorway.

"Come outside, Virginia. It's so hot in here."

They sat beside the lane under the wild plum trees. Her thin, nervous fingers pulled up the dry grass and crushed it to bits. David's voice was gentle.

"What's the matter, Virginia? You haven't been happy for a long time."

91

"Oh, David, I don't know. It's not anything I can talk about."

"Any problem is easier when we share it with someone. Don't you trust me?" Virginia looked up in astonishment.

"Oh, yes, I trust you, David. Ever since you came back from Omaha, it's been so wonderful. We've had such good talks. You've told me so many things I'd been wondering about, things I couldn't ask anyone."

"Well, then why not tell me about this?"

"We-e-l-l, I want to join the church." There, it was out.

"Why, that's wonderful," David breathed.

"No, it isn't! I can't! I don't have the price!"

David spat out the grass stem he was chewing and looked at her through the gathering darkness in astonishment. "Virginia, I don't know what you're talking about. You know it doesn't cost money to join the church."

"Yes, it does." Virginia struggled to keep her voice even. "Dunker women wear bonnets to show that they're apart from the world. A bonnet costs a dollar and I don't have any way to get that much money. I—I tried to earn it, but—it rained and—and—and the skunk killed the hen, and . . ." Virginia dropped her head in her hands, the hot tears flowing.

David gave a muffled exclamation and put his arms around her. After a long moment he spoke. "Thank you for telling me, Virgie." He fished in his pocket. "Here. Please take this. One reason I came back from Omaha was to be closer to the family so I could help out, and I can't think of another way I'd rather help." He dropped a worn silver dollar into her hands. "And here, how about this?" Virginia felt the welcome folds of his handkerchief.

"Thanks," she said, dabbing at her eyes. "But, David, that's two days' hard work for you."

"Like I said, I can't think of a better thing to spend it for." They sat quietly a few minutes, listening to the shrill cicada chorus in the hot night. Then David spoke again, gently.

"Virgie, I have to go now. May I drive around by Brother

Hersler's and tell him you'll be baptized next Sunday? I'd love to." Virginia nodded, not trusting herself to speak.

"Bless you, Dear," David whispered and got to his feet.

Virginia sat quietly in the dark, hearing the harness jingle as he drove past her to the end of the lane and turned north over the hill. Then she heard his voice, brought to her by the night wind, "Praise God from Whom all blessings flow, Praise Him, all creatures . . ." Her heart contracted.

"Oh, God, thank You for David, and my family and friends, and everything . . ." Her prayer merged with the echo of the ancient chant, "Praise Father, Son, and Holy Ghost."

Chapter 14.
"NOT WITH BRAIDED HAIR"

Virginia thought maybe Brother Hersler would keep her news a secret and surprise the congregation on Sunday. But on Wednesday she walked to town for the mail and met Sister Miller on the street.

"Virginia, dear, I heard you're going to be baptized on Sunday and I'm so glad for you. We're so happy to have you and David in the church," Sister Miller said warmly, putting an arm around Virginia's shoulders.

"Thank you, Sister Miller. I'm happy about it, too." A good warm feeling spread over Virginia. Now she would really belong and could take part in Love Feast and everything. Sister Miller looked as if she wanted to say something more, but she just smiled and pressed Virginia's hand again before they separated.

On Thursday John and Alice Streeter drove over in the evening. John told Virginia in his sincere way how happy he was for her decision. Now that he no longer made her so uneasy, Virginia could see why David liked him so much. His handshake was warm and friendly.

When John went to chat with Mike at the barn, Alice said, "Virginia, would you like to go home with us after church on Sunday? I'll help you get ready for the baptism and you can go to the river with us."

"Oh, that would be fine, Alice. I—I don't know quite what to do. There's no one here but Pearl, and she's not a member . . . " Virginia's voice trailed away.

"Of course. I know just how you feel, and we'd think it a great privilege to help in any way we could."

"I've been wondering," Virginia said hesitantly, "about my bonnet. I have the money," she added hastily, "but I was in Shrevesville yesterday and didn't see any Dunker women wear."

"Oh, yes," Alice replied warmly. "I got mine at David City. John's been saying he must go down there on business. I'll just ask him if he can't go tomorrow. We could go along and get you all fixed up."

"That would be wonderful," Virginia breathed in relief. All the time she'd been worrying about the money for her bonnet she hadn't thought about such details as actually buying it.

Alice helped her choose a plain, black bonnet that tied under the chin. It wasn't made from shiny cloth like Alice's was, but then Lottie had said Alice spent more than a dollar for hers.

Afterward Virginia remembered Sunday, August 23, 1896, as a day of great joy, but the details were hazy. All she remembered about going to the Platte was watching the horses snatch sunflowers to eat as they walked along the hot, dusty road. The large, yellow blossoms jerked and bobbed as the horses ate down to them. That was a silly thing to remember. Horses always did that.

The Platte was lower than at David's baptism in the spring. There were more sand bars above the water, and Brother Hersler had to wade out farther to find a pool deep enough. Virginia was surprised to discover that there were several other applicants for baptism. Apparently John's sincerity and persistance had gotten results.

Again Brother Miller led the hymns, as he had last spring. "I'm not ashamed to own my Lord, Or to defend his cause," the congregation sang as Virginia began the long walk to Brother Hersler. She couldn't see clearly as she returned to the bank, but she felt the love of her family and friends around her. Her father's face was wet with tears when he kissed her and David's hand pressed hard on her arm. Pearl and Lottie waited their turn to embrace her.

Early in September the church would celebrate the Love Feast. Virginia knew this was a high point in church life and she had always wished she could take part. Now that she was a member she was looking forward to it with great joy. Everyone always testified of the great blessings they received at Love Feast. There were many preparations to be made as people came from other Dunker churches to share in the service. The old schoolhouse where they had church was too small, so a large tent would be placed in the yard.

Love Feast would be on Saturday night, with "all-day preaching"—or three services—the next day. There was much discussion of plans at church on the preceding Sunday.

Virginia walked up to a group of women around Sister Miller and was astounded when they suddenly stopped talking. Sister Miller smiled at her nervously and Virginia, embarrassed, walked on. Later, as she stood with the young people, she noticed those same women whispering and nodding toward her. Goodness, Virginia thought, are they talking about me? I can't imagine why.

Pearl was "working out" at the neighbor's after a new baby's arrival that week, so Virginia was alone on Thursday when Sister Miller came. She chatted nervously for awhile, not like her usual friendly self.

Finally she said, "Virginia, I was—was wondering if you'd like to—to come over to my house tomorrow afternoon." I thought I—I could help you with your hair," she finished in a rush, fingering her dress nervously. "That is, if you want me to."

"Of course, Sister Miller, but I don't understand. Is there something wrong with it?"

"Well, Dear, I know you have no mother to explain these things, and you know how men are," she added with a nervous laugh. "They never notice anything. But you know, the Dunkers are plain people, and now that you've joined the church, well, you really should not braid your hair any longer."

"I shouldn't?" Virginia asked in amazement. "Well, I guess no one at church wears their hair in a braid except the little girls, but I just thought that was because they were older. I didn't know it had anything to do with belonging to the church."

"Well, you know we're a New Testament church," Sister Miller's voice sounded relieved to be talking like a Sunday School teacher. "Paul has quite a bit to say about women's hair. In First Timothy two he says women should not braid their hair."

"Oh, my, Sister Miller. I didn't know," Breathed Virginia.

"Of course, Dear. I was sure you wouldn't mind if I told you. I'd be glad to help you put it up tomorrow. Then you could wear it up for Love Feast." Sister Miller stepped into the buggy and picked up the reins.

"That would be very nice. I'll be there. And thank you so much."

Virginia stood by the lane after the buggy had disappeared over the ridge, her thoughts whirling. My goodness, there's a lot more to joining the church than I thought. Is that why the women were talking about me Sunday? I didn't know Dunker women shouldn't braid their hair. I always thought it was a neat, plain way to wear it. Well, I'm sure the church knows best. And it will be fun to wear it like a grown-up.

All evening and the next morning these thoughts continued. Virginia found the verse Sister Miller had referred to. "In like manner also, that women adorn themselves in modest apparel, with shamefacedness and sobriety; not with braided hair, or gold, or pearls, or costly array."

Of course it was wrong to spend money on luxuries of jewelry and fine clothes. And she didn't mind being dressed in sobriety, but why should she be shamefaced? What was wrong with being a woman? Oh, well, she wouldn't worry about it. It was nice of Sister Miller to want to help her.

Still underneath was always the nagging feeling that she wasn't good enough the way she was, braid and all.

By the time Virginia had walked to the Miller home, she'd convinced herself that it would be fun to wear her hair up. After all, Lottie had worn hers up as long as Virginia had known her. Wouldn't the girls at school be surprised when she went back next week? Of course she wouldn't wear it all loose and waved, the way they did, but at least it would be up.

Sister Miller welcomed her warmly, but Virginia was glad that the children were outside and Brother Miller and the older boys were raking the third cutting of hay on the back forty. She couldn't stand to have anyone watching this.

While Virginia unbraided her long hair, Sister Miller opened a folded tissue paper lying on the table. Inside was a new prayer covering, made of stiff, white net with long streamers to tie under the chin. Oh, my goodness, I forgot all about a prayer veil, thought Virginia. I wonder how much they cost? I spent all the money on my bonnet.

"Here's your prayer veil, Virginia. I hope it's the right size. We'll try it on after we fix your hair."

"Should—should I buy it?" Virginia asked faintly.

"Oh, no. It's part of my job as deacon's wife to provide prayer veils for the new converts. We're just so glad to have you," Sister Miller smiled warmly as she picked up the brush.

It felt different to have someone else working with her hair. Virginia had been braiding it herself ever since she started to school. Now, as Sister Miller brushed and combed it in different directions than it was used to going, it seemed to have a mind of its own. The curved, brown pins didn't hold it, but popped out as soon as they were put in.

Time after time Sister Miller patiently brushed, combed and wrapped the long hair in a knot at the back of Virginia's head, patted it and at last placed the large pins to hold it. Each time the pins popped out and the hair fell down. Finally, they got a basin of water and wet the brush.

The cool water felt good on Virginia's hot skin, but now when her hair fell down it was stringy instead of a soft, fluffy brown cloud. At first they had laughed as the hair came tumbling down, but after several tries it wasn't so funny.

As Sister Miller grew more anxious, Virginia became more embarrassed. There must be something wrong with her. Even her hair wouldn't do what it was supposed to. Her only consolation was that no one else was around, but suddenly she heard the rattle of harness in the yard.

"Oh, no," Virginia breathed.

"Never mind. You just stay right here. I'll go see who it is and try to get rid of them. You wet it some more. Maybe that's what it needs. For a minute there I thought it was going to stay." Sister Miller hurried out.

Virginia shrank into a corner, so no one could see her through the window. It was stifling in the house and her hair was so hot. If only she could just braid it and go home, but she couldn't wear it this way to Love Feast, and she couldn't miss such an important occasion the first time she was allowed to go!

Suddenly she heard voices! Surely Sister Miller wasn't bringing someone into the house! But there in the doorway stood Elder Peters' wife. Virginia didn't know her very well. She always had her mouth pinched shut as if she knew the young people were up to no good. Now her mouth got even tighter as she listened to Sister Miller's explanation.

"Well, *I'll* make it stay up," Sister Peters said firmly. Striding across the kitchen, she seized the comb and raked it through Virginia's hair. Ouch! Sister Miller's hands had felt different, but at least they had been gentle. Sister Peters' rough hands caught in the hair and pulled while Virginia tried not to wince. It would never do to be a coward. Sister Peters brushed and combed, skinning the hair back so hard that Virginia's eyes felt like slits. She was sure she'd never be able to open them normally. The tears rolled down her cheeks as Sister Peters jabbed the sharp pins into Virginia's scalp—straight in, it felt like. At last, when Virginia's head felt like a tight, shiny pincushion stuck full of pins, Sister Peters stood back with her arms akimbo and said, "There!"

Was it up at last? Virginia took a deep breath of relief—and all the pins popped out. In the silence she could hear them hitting the floor with little clicks.

"Oh, dear," sobbed Virginia, "maybe I shouldn't go to Love Feast," but her heart sank as she said it. She'd waited so long and wanted so much to feel that she belonged. Was she still going to have to stay on the outside?

"Oh, no, Virginia. We want you to come." Sister Miller looked as if she'd been crying. Her hands twisted nervously.

"Don't worry. It'll stay. Get me some soap," Sister Peters said grimly.

"Oh! Do you think . . . ?" Sister Miller gasped.

"That'll do it. Just get me some."

Sister Miller left the room. Virginia wished she could crawl into a hole and die. She must be a nobody who had to be made over completely before she could belong to the church. Sister Miller acted as if she were sorry about the whole thing, but it was clear that Sister Peters wouldn't stop now.

Sister Miller came back with a bar of strong yellow laundry soap, made in a big black kettle from lard and lye. "I was sure I had some castille," she said apologetically, "but I guess I gave it to Mrs. Swift for her baby. This is all I have."

"And it's good enough for anybody. Just hand it here," Sister Peters said firmly.

Dipping the soap in the basin of water, she used it as a brush, soaping the hair until it was hard and stiff, skinning it back until Virginia felt as if her face and head were held by a vise. She'd never be able to move them again. Tears squeezed out of her closed eyes as Sister Peters again roughly coiled the long, stiff hair around Virginia's head and jabbed the pins in even harder than before. Then, one hand still holding the hair in place, she reached for the prayer veil Sister Miller handed her. Carefully she fitted the cap over Virginia's coiled hair, but before she could tie the strings, the pins sprang out again as if alive and the hair tumbled down in stiff, hard strings around Virginia's face.

There was a shout outside. "Oh, no," gasped Sister Miller, and left the room.

"I guess that's Elder Peters," said his wife. "We noticed Brother Miller in the back forty when we came, so Sam went back to talk to him about putting up the tent for tomorrow night while I came in."

Shame flooded over Virginia. This whole thing was degrading enough, just among women. She couldn't possibly let a man see her like this and certainly not the elder! Everyone knew how strict Elder Peters was. Would this nightmare never stop? Couldn't she just wake up and realize it was a horrible dream? But no. She could hear them on the back step, Sister Miller explaining nervously what had happened. "She thinks maybe she shouldn't come to Love Feast," Sister Miller finished.

A shadow fell across the floor and Elder Peters stood in the doorway. He looked at his wife, red-faced and perspiring. He looked at Virginia, shrinking behind her ugly hair, too embarrassed to raise her red eyes. He had already seen Sister Miller's sympathetic tears. In the silence Virginia could hear a cricket somewhere outside.

Elder Peters walked slowly to the center of the room. "Wirchie is coming to Love Feast." Virginia had never heard him say her name before. He softened the "g" sound and mixed his "w's" and "v's" the way Father said the older people did back in the East. "And Wirchie vill vear her hair in a braid down her back the vay she alvays has."

"But, Sam . . . " began Sister Peters.

"Myrtle!" said Elder Peters sternly. He put his hand gently on Virginia's sweaty arm. "Ve are glad to have you in the church, child. I shall expect you tomorrow night at Love Feast. Come, Mother." Taking Sister Peters' arm, he ushered her out of the house before she could say another word. The harness rattled as they drove out of the farmyard.

Numbly Virginia reached for the comb and brush, the ugly yellow soap and the basin of water and carried them to the dry sink. She didn't want to talk or see the sympathy on Sister Miller's face.

"Oh, Virginia, dear, I'm so sorry about all this. I should have remembered that braided hair needs longer than one day to get used to another style. Do come to Love Feast just the way you are. It'll be all right." She hesitated. "I'm afraid your hair will have to be washed. I'd be glad to help you with it, but I think the children will be coming in pretty soon . . . " her voice trailed away.

"That's all right, Sister Miller. I'll just go on along home. I'll have time to wash it before supper, I think." If she could just get away before the tears came!

Sister Miller gave her a shawl to put over her head, but it was so hot Virginia took it off as soon as she was out of sight. No use to get soap all over a wool shawl. Besides, if anyone saw her with her head covered on this hot day they'd think she was crazy. However, Virginia was determined no one would see her. She cut across fields and pastures whenever she could, running at top speed along the roads, the dust settling on the stiff, damp strings of her hair.

Virginia was nearly sick from heat and emotion when she finally reached the safety of her own farmyard. Running dizzily into the house, she slumped into a chair to get her breath. As her head cleared she saw a note on the table.

"Virgey, I tuk sum food to the feeld as we must get the hey cut tonite. We'll werk lait and chor when we cum in. Pa."

Virginia smiled faintly. Poor Father! He's a fine man, but he never learned to spell. At least that means they won't be here at supper time. It's four o'clock now. If I sit in the sun my hair'll be dry enough to cover up when I have to do the chicken chores. I'll do as much of the other work as I can, too, and have a hot supper waiting when they come in.

Carrying the dishpan and water to the bench on the back step, Virginia rinsed her hair many times before the soap washed out. The cool water felt good, but the soap stung terribly. Some of her tears were because her eyes hurt, but most were for the deep humiliation she felt. If she could only erase this afternoon from her mind and never remember it again!

The next day Virginia tried to think of an excuse for not attending Love Feast, but there was none. Elder Peters was expecting her and Sister Miller would be so disappointed if she didn't go. So she went, but the great blessings she'd expected escaped her. She was terribly conscious of that braid down her back and was certain everyone there was remembering Paul's admonition, "not with braided hair." I was sure everything would be different when I joined the church, she thought disappointedly, but I guess I'm still the same old me—with even more problems than before.

Chapter 15.
NOTHING PASSES FRANK

The dishes finished, Virginia picked up the kerosene lamp and carried it from the warm kitchen to her chilly bedroom. She and Mike were going to revival meetings at Edholm and she wanted to be ready when he came in from choring. Setting the map on her dresser, Virginia peered into the cloudy mirror above it. Her hair looked a little strubbly; she really ought to redo it. With practiced fingers she took out the pins, brushed and rewound the long coil.

During the week between Love Feast and the beginning of school, Virginia had grimly attacked her hair, pinning it up again and again until it finally stayed. By the time the next Sunday came, it managed to stay up all during church and when school started Maggie Peterson had complimented her on how nice it looked.

Now Virginia leaned into the mirror, wondering if she dared soften the hair above her widow's peak. When she pulled it back tight, it accented the high, wide forehead above her deepset eyes.

As she turned to change her dress, Virginia's eyes fell on the United States map, hanging beside the dresser. It had come back from Omaha all in one piece, with no prize—as Mr. Vining had said. But it was an honor to think that it had hung in the Exposition all summer, with people from all over the world seeing it.

When she was dressed, Virginia carried the lamp back to the kitchen again, so Mike could have it when he came in.

In the hall she noticed a long cobweb she had missed on cleaning day. Oh, well, that'll be seed for next time, she grinned to herself. Pearl was "working out" almost all the time now, first for one neighbor woman and then another, so that left the housework for Virginia to do after school and on weekends. There was a lot that wasn't getting done, but Father never complained when she had to let things go in the house. Now that the fall work was finished he would be in the house more and he was such good help.

When Mike had changed clothes and gone to bring up the horse, Virginia went out to wait for him in the clear November night. The ground had frozen slightly, but there was no snow. Overhead myriads of stars twinkled in the clear sky. Virginia was surprised to see that Mike was bringing Frank and the two-wheeled road cart. The cart was nice for trips to town when you didn't need to haul too many people or too much weight. Mike was proud of the new road cart and of Frank, an old race horse he had just bought.

Sitting beside Mike, carefully holding the two songbooks they always took with them to church, Virginia remembered the night she and David had walked to revival meeting. Was that less than a year ago? So much had happened since then, it seemed much longer. She felt so much older and happier. It was hard now to remember how miserable she'd been all summer. Maybe she shouldn't have been so shy about telling someone she needed money for a bonnet. And her face still burned with shame when she remembered that humiliating afternoon at Sister Miller's home, but she supposed Sister Miller had been sincerely trying to help her.

Anyway, that was over and at last Virginia was beginning to feel at home in the church as she'd always wanted to. One thing that had helped had been going to District Meeting at Juniata, Nebraska, last month with Pearl, David and some of the other young people. The messages had been inspiring and it was so much fun to meet people from other churches. There had been a large group of young people there, and they had enjoyed some great fellowship between services.

One of their leaders had been Ira Snavely, Nebraska's youngest preacher. He told them about his experiences at Moody Bible Institute in Chicago and offered many challenges that really made them think. Virginia felt very grown-up and serious as she listened to him.

Now as Virginia and Mike rolled along in the crisp, beautiful night, she relaxed and enjoyed the feeling of being young and having some place to go. This was her last year of high school. She was learning to manage the housework alone—with Father's help, of course—and she was becoming more at ease with others, though she was still more shy than she wanted to be. She didn't know what the future held after graduation next spring, but for tonight she wasn't going to worry about it.

Edholm was six miles away, but with Frank's steady gait they arrived in good time. Virginia waited on the church steps while Mike tied Frank and covered him with a blanket so he wouldn't chill.

After the service the people lingered on the steps, talking and laughing. Finally they broke into families, groups of young people or couples and went to their buggies. It had clouded up during the meeting and the stars were gone. When the church lamps were blown out it was pitch dark. Talking to their horses, or calling to each other, many of the congregation moved in a long line of buggies down the dark road.

Mike and Virginia were near the end of the line, but someone behind them was in a hurry and turned out to pass the line. As he passed them, Mike gave a sudden exclamation and gripped the lines, but it was too late. Frank—the old race horse—had been trained never to let anything pass him. With a great lunge, he turned out of the line and followed the buggy ahead.

Virginia gasped. Dropping the songbooks, she clutched Mike's left arm with one hand and the low outer rim of the road cart with the other, hanging on with all her strength.

The buggy Frank was trying to pass couldn't turn back in, so two galloping horses passed rig after rig in the long line. As they whizzed past, the wind whistling in their ears, Virginia was dimly aware of dark shapes and pale blurs of faces. She could feel Mike's muscles straining in his desperate struggle to keep Frank under control.

Suddenly Virginia remembered the culvert ahead. The road wasn't wide enough at the culvert for two buggies, even if it weren't too dark to see where the edge was. I was so happy an hour ago, she thought. Is this the end? If we upset, we'll be thrown out and terribly hurt or . . . As they approached the culvert Virginia could feel Mike leaning toward his side of the cart, nearer the center of the road. She leaned with him and felt the jolt of the outer wheel as it hit the road again after riding in thin air across the ditch.

After a time that seemed forever, the buggy ahead reached the head of the line. Quickly the driver pulled his horse over and slowed him to walk. Frank continued galloping until he was well ahead, then turned in to the right side of the road, still demanding every ounce of Mike's strength to hold him.

When they finally turned off the main road, Mike was able to slow Frank down somewhat. Only then did he speak. "Are you all right, Virgie?"

"I—I guess so, Mike. Are you?" Virginia breathed shakily.

"My shoulders will ache tomorrow, but I'm all in one piece."

Virginia loosened her stiff fingers and felt around in the dark. "I guess we lost our songbooks."

"I'm sorry. I'll buy us some more."

"Oh, don't be in a hurry. Maybe we'll find them."

"It was my fault," Mike said. "I knew Frank wouldn't let anything pass him. We shoulda waited until all the buggies going south had left. He whipped out before I realized what he was doing."

"Well, it's all over now, Mike, and we're not hurt. Will Frank be all right?"

107

"I'll rub him down good and he'll be all right. He really can run, can't he?"

"Yes, and he wants everyone to know it," Virginia laughed faintly.

Mike pulled up to the barn door before he stopped Frank. Then he climbed down and helped Virginia out. "Can you make it to the house? It'll take me awhile to care for Frank."

"Of course I can," Virginia said, but she was surprised to find that her legs felt like cooked noodles. Slowly she made her way to the house and sat down weakly on the kitchen daybed. Well, I guess life always has something else waiting, she thought. Worries, troubles, excitement or danger— there's always something to break the monotony when you think everything is going smoothly. Tomorrow is a school day, and I'll be perfectly happy to walk there on my own two legs, if they'll hold me by then.

Chapter 16.
MEMORIES

Mike was upset. Virginia didn't know why, but as she and the girls bustled around putting Sunday dinner on the table, she could tell something was wrong. Mike sat in the corner with a troubled face. Father must know about it, too, for he was very quiet, not laughing and joking as usual.

Pearl was between housekeeping jobs right now. Elizabeth and David were also home for the day, so once again the family, except for Katie, was together. Katie's little Harry was just a few weeks old, so of course they wouldn't be seeing her again until summer.

The February day was bitterly cold, and the family was glad to stay around the stove in the kitchen. When the table was cleared, Virginia brought out the autograph album she had received for Christmas. It was a beautiful wine-red plush, with "Autographs" written in gold on the cover. She hated to think how much Pearl had taken from her school fund to buy it, but it was so nice to be able to exchange autographs at school. Several of her teachers had already written inspiring sentiments. Now she wanted Elizabeth and David to add theirs.

As she handed the book to David, Mike crossed his legs and mumbled something under his breath. "All right, Mike," Father sighed. He cleared his throat and said, "Since we're all together, there's something I believe we should talk about. It really concerns all of us. Mr. and Mrs. Jake Ruth talked to me today about—about something they must have given a lot of thought to."

109

"Well, what was it? Why all the mystery?" Elizabeth asked impatiently.

Father's hands were clasping and unclasping. "They—they want to take Virginia."

David dropped the album on the table with a thud. "Take Virginia? You mean adopt her?"

Father swallowed.

"Well, they wouldn't actually adopt her, I guess, but they'd want to think of her as their own. They said they'd give her a good education."

There was a shocked silence in the kitchen. Virginia stood stock still. Leave Father? Leave the family? Of course as they grew older they began "working out," but they were all, except Katie, right here in the community and saw each other often. How could she belong to someone else? Dimly she heard the others begin to talk as the first shock of the idea wore off.

"Virginia's so smart. She would make good use of a fine education," said Elizabeth.

"The Ruths have no children, but quite a prosperous farm. Virginia would have many things there we couldn't give her," added Pearl. Virginia remembered how disappointed Pearl had been last spring when she couldn't go to Institute.

"Well, you sound as if you couldn't wait to get rid of me," she cried. "Father, do you want me to go to?"

Father's face was strained as he looked up at her. "No, Virgie, I don't, but it's selfish of me to hold you back when they could give you so many more opportunities. I've been hoping times would get better, but . . ."

"No!" Mike said loudly and harshly. The others stared at him.

"Well, Mike, they really could give her more opportunities. You know that," Elizabeth said decidedly.

"She mustn't go," Mike stated stubbornly, his hands twisting. "I—I promised Mother."

The room was silent again. Suddenly Virginia remembered the day just a year ago when they had listened to Fa-

110

ther's war stories. She sat down on the daybed beside Father and put her hand on his arm.

"Tell me about Mother," she said softly. "I remember a little about baby Elmer's funeral. That was a month after Mother died, wasn't it? All I can remember about Mother is the time I sat beside her on the stool and had soup while she ate hers in the rocking chair. Remember, Father, when I was just a little girl and asked you what kind of soup it was?"

"Yes. I couldn't believe you remembered it, you were so young."

"Was Mother bedfast for a long time?" asked Virginia.

"No, but she was ailing before Elmer was born," Mike replied.

"He was her ninth child. The other little ones died back in Virginia," murmured David.

"She was singing hymns in bed before it grew light that day," said Father. "I thought then that she . . ." his voice broke, ". . . she was pretty close to heaven," he finished in a whisper. Virginia swallowed against the lump in her throat and pressed his hand.

Mike rose and noisily dumped more wood into the cookstove. "I'd always heard that if the doves land on the window sill where someone is ill, it means the person will pass away. So when Mother didn't get up that last morning, I stayed handy to keep the doves away from the window, but—they did land once," he finished gruffly, sitting down again.

"When Mother called us all in to the bedside, we couldn't find Elizabeth. Father told me to go and find her, but I was so worried I didn't look very hard. I've always been sorry about that, Lizzie," David said to her softly.

"I'm sorry I ran away and hid," Elizabeth answered so quietly they could barely hear her, "but I was so frightened."

"In another month she would have been thirty-six," Father sighed.

"After she died, some people took us three little girls to

111

their house and made us new dresses while we were asleep," Pearl said suddenly. "I didn't know I remembered that!"

"Anyway, we had prayer beside her bed and she asked us older ones to keep the family together. And I promised," Mike repeated.

Virginia stared at him. She'd always thought Mike was only interested in work and his horses. She'd been sure many times that he didn't understand her, but only wanted to tease. Was that just to cover up what he really felt, but couldn't say? I wonder if we ever really know people, even when we live with them, she thought. It was a new idea.

"What did you tell the Ruths, Father?" she asked.

Father rubbed his hand across his forehead as if he'd forgotten where he was. "I told them we'd have to think about it."

"Well, you must tell them it was very kind to offer, but I can't leave all of you. You're my family! We've stayed together this long, and I'm certainly not going to leave the nest now!"

"But, Virginia, it would be a good way to get an education and, after all, the rest of us are working away, so we're really not together any more," Elizabeth argued.

"But it would be different if I went to live with the Ruths as their child. I suppose I'd enjoy going to college, but I'm sure there's plenty of time for that, after I've earned the privilege," Virginia laughed. "I don't know what will open up after graduation, but I guess something will. There'll always be work here at home, that's sure."

Later Virginia found herself alone in the kitchen with David. She'd been exploring her new ideas about Mike. Her eyes blurred every time she thought about a sixteen-year-old boy guarding his mother's window to keep the doves away.

"David, I was wondering something about Mike. You know he's almost thirty and that's awfully old. Well, I think it's old," she added defensively as she saw the ghost of a smile on David's face. "Do you think his promise to Mother is why he hasn't married? He never takes a girl

112

anywhere or even talks to one, as far as I can see. Do you think he's giving that up for us?"

"It might be, Virginia. I know he's taken his responsibility as the oldest very seriously. But I wouldn't write him off completely. Thirty isn't quite as old as you might think!"

Chapter 17.
THE SOUL'S SINCERE DESIRE

"That certainly was a fine Bible study tonight, Brother Hersler," said Lottie one Friday evening as she and Virginia paused on the steps of the church.

"I'm glad you enjoy our teachers' meetings, girls. It's a real joy to have you young folks taking such an active interest in the church. Taking your Sunday afternoons to distribute tracts in David City and Schuyler shows how dedicated you are," Brother Hersler answered sincerely.

"We have to be missionaries in our own way. We can't all go to India. I guess we'll be here every night for revival meetings for the next two weeks, won't we?" said Lottie.

"Yes," Virginia sighed, shifting her Bible to the other arm. "I don't know how I'll get it all in. I almost feel I shouldn't take time to go to David City with you tomorrow."

"Oh, Virginia, Please!" Lottie pleaded. "It'll be such fun! I really don't have too much to do, so we should get home early. I'm eager to see my pictures. It was just dear of Seth and Morris to give me the money for them. But it won't be half as much fun if you don't go."

"Oh, I want to go all right. We haven't had an outing for awhile. I could just forget about cleaning and studies for once."

The next day was March at its best. Spring sang in the air as Lottie, Virginia and Lottie's sister Mayme drove mer-

114

rily toward David City in the buggy. Lottie had had her picture taken and was going to pick up the finished photos from the photographer. The five dollar bill that Seth had given her was tucked securely into her pocket book.

In David City the girls did a few errands and a little shopping, then decided to have dinner before they got the pictures. After lunch they walked gaily down the street, eager to see the pictures of Lottie in her best dress and bonnet.

At the photographer's Lottie reached confidently into her purse for the money, but it was gone. She looked again carefully, then frantically took everything out of her purse, checking every corner where it might have slipped. The bill was simply not there.

"Oh, what will I do?" Lottie asked heart brokenly. "Seth and Morris worked so hard to pay for my pictures. I just *can't* have lost it!"

"There must be something we can do," murmured Virginia.

"You girls go back to the cafe and see if it's there," Lottie said decidedly. "I'm going into the dressing room and pray that God will help us find it."

Virginia and Mayme retraced their steps to the restaurant, scanning the sidewalk as they went.

"Oh, we just have to find it," said Mayme, as they entered. "Look, that's the boy who served us. We'll ask him."

"Excuse us," Virginia said hesitantly, as the waiter looked up. "We—we just ate here and now we—we've lost some money. Did—did you see any?"

"It was fi—five dollars, a bill," Mayme said quickly.

The boy reached into his pocket and pulled out a five-dollar bill. "This was under the table where you were eating. I found it when I swept the floor." He held it out to them.

"Oh, thank you. Thank you so very much," Virginia and Mayme said together. Outside the restaurant they hurried back to the photographer's shop, calling, "Lottie, Lottie!" as they burst in.

Lottie came from behind the curtain of the dressing room. "Did you find it?" She asked anxiously.

"The boy found it when he was sweeping the floor." Mayme held out the bill.

Quickly they paid the photographer and took the precious pictures with them. On the sidewalk again they opened the package, and there was Lottie looking back soberly at them from the picture. Her face was all that was visible below her best black bonnet. The high collar of her dark dress rose above the velvet ribbons that tied the bonnet beneath her slightly pointed chin. Her clear eyes, above her straight nose and full lips, stared pensively into space.

"Oh, Lottie, how good it is of you," Virginia breathed.

"Yes, but we wouldn't have the pictures if that boy hadn't been honest. "I'll always thank God for that," breathed Lottie fervently.

The girls drove home, chatting of many things. As they neared Virginia's home Lottie said, "Virginia, it's been such a long time since you've stayed overnight with me. Can't you come home with me next Wednesday after meeting? You could go to school from our house the next morning."

"That would be fine. Let's plan it for then," replied Virginia, as the buggy stopped in her yard.

On Wednesday after the service, Lottie and Virginia picked up their songbooks and settled their shawls around them against the chill March wind. Soon they had reached the shelter of Lottie's home.

"Lottie, there's something I'm very concerned about," Virginia said, when they were in the privacy of Lottie's room. "You know I joined the church last summer and it's been such a joy to me. Father said once it was my mother's great concern that all of us join the church. Yesterday we got a letter from Katie. She and George have joined the Methodist church there in Douglas, where they live."

"Oh, that's wonderful, Virginia," said Lottie sincerely, taking down her hair to braid it for the night.

"Yes, we're happy for her, but it made me think. Here we're having revival meetings again at our church, and

116

there are still three in our family who haven't joined. Pearl said something the last time she was home that made me think she's considering it. I don't know about Elizabeth, but I keep thinking about Mike. Somehow I've come to feel so much closer to Mike this winter. I keep remembering our runaway last November and how serious it could have been if Mike hadn't handled Frank so well."

"It certainly could have been," said Lottie, "and I meant to ask you at church tonight. Aren't those songbooks the ones you lost?"

"Yes. They were thrown out when we crossed the culvert, but someone from Edholm found them right afterwards and returned them to us not long ago."

"I'm glad you got them back, but I didn't mean to change the subject," Lottie said seriously. "I know what you mean about Mike. I joined the church several years ago, but my brother Morris hasn't. He and I are great pals, you know, and I guess I should say something to him, but I haven't yet. For one thing, he can't attend many of the meetings since he's going to the Academy down at David City."

"Won't he get home Friday night in time to come?" Virginia asked as she slipped into her long flannel nightgown.

"Yes, but just going on weekends might not be enough."

"Lottie, do—do you think we could pray for them?" Virginia asked shyly.

"Yes, Virginia, I think we should. I'm sure God helped us last Saturday."

On their knees beside the bed, Lottie and Virginia prayed sincerely for Morris and Mike, asking that they would be open to God's spirit and that His will would be done in their lives. Then, much relieved, they climbed into bed and chatted until sleep came.

On Friday Virginia was surprised to see Lottie waiting for her on the church steps, though everyone else had gone in. "Oh, Virgie, I've just got to tell you something."

"My goodness, Lottie, what is it? The service is about to start, I'm sure."

"I know, but I just have to tell you. I'm so happy! You

know Morris came home from school tonight. I asked him, as I usually do, how the week went at school. He said, "Oh, I don't know what was the matter, but Wednesday night I was so restless and couldn't sleep. I couldn't figure out why.'"

"He did? Why, Lottie, Wednesday night was when we prayed for him and Mike!"

"I know! I didn't tell him about it, but doesn't it look to you as if God heard our prayers? That was why Morris couldn't sleep!"

"Oh, Lottie, it could have been! Isn't that wonderful? Let's continue our prayers for the boys and see what God can do."

Before the revival was over, Morris, Mike and Pearl announced their intention to be baptized and join the church. In the whole congregation, no one was happier than Virginia and Lottie.

Chapter 18.
ADVENTURES WITH HORSES

"Virginia, would you like to go to Teacher's Institute with me this summer?" Pearl asked, placing the spoon holder in the center of the table. "Since I'm home today I thought we should talk to Father about it, but I wanted to ask you first."

"But, Pearl, you know that takes money, and I haven't any," Virginia said, amazed, as she stirred the gravy.

"Well, I've been 'working out' almost all winter. Sometimes I got a dollar and a half a week, but some people paid me three."

"Really? I didn't know you got that much for 'working out.' Ouch!" Virginia burned her finger on the hot spoon. "But, even so, that's not enough to pay for both of us, is it?"

"Yes, I think we can do it if we're not too extravagant. If we pass the exams and get a certificate, we'll see if we can get schools to teach next fall."

To Virginia's surprise Father favored Pearl's suggestion, though he sighed at the thought of the youngest leaving home.

"But how will you manage all the work?" Virginia asked.

"Oh, come now, Virgie, you forget that I was batching years ago when you folks lived in Kansas," laughed Mike, piling mashed potatoes on his plate for the third time. "Mother always said, 'Soda biscuits and spuds with the skins on and store tea and molasses cake is the Nebraskans' diet.' I can manage most of that and Father can make the cake."

"Oh, I'm not worried about the cooking. Father's a good cook, and of course he does most of the gardening, too. But there's a lot more to be done around here, believe it or not! What about the chicken chores? Who'll do them?" Virginia asked.

"By the end of June the little chicks'll be pretty well able to care for themselves. We'll manage somehow if you want to go, Virgie. Do you?" Father asked wistfully, spearing another piece of fried ham.

"Well, I don't know, Father. This is all so sudden! It's true I'd like to get some more education, and if I were teaching I could be earning some money. It's about time I began pulling my own weight around here."

"Oh, Virgie, Virgie. You mustn't talk that way! You've always done your share. This is a good chance Pearl's offering you and I think you ought to take it. When doors open for us we should walk through them, even if we don't know where they will take us." Father smiled at Virginia lovingly, his beard working as he chewed.

Graduation came and went in a daze. Virginia discovered it was much more fun to tell her classmates she'd be going to Institute than it had been to say she'd be staying home. Several of them would attend also and would share rides back and forth to David City.

The early summer was busy and happy. In addition to housework, Virginia had to prepare clothes for school. Ordinarily she didn't have many summer dresses, as everyone spent long days in the fields and there weren't many places to go. Alice Streeter and Lottie helped her with the sewing. Virginia found out it wasn't the horrible job she'd thought when she was younger and the dressmaker made all their clothes.

One hot day near the end of May, storm clouds suddenly boiled up from the northwest. Virginia ran out to shut up the little chicks and be sure the coops were not sitting where the water would wash badly. Getting back to the house just as the first raindrops were pelting the dusty farmyard, she began closing windows against the storm.

Above the wind, she heard the rhythmic pat-a-pat a-pat of a horse coming very fast down the hill. Running to the door, she peered out through the rain. Yes, it was Frank, but *Father* was in the road cart! Oh, dear, she thought, Father isn't nearly the horseman that Mike is, and Frank's coming so fast! Will he slow down when he turns into the lane? There's nothing to hang onto in the road cart. "Oh, please, don't let Father be hurt!" she prayed.

Her heart pounding rapidly and her hands clasped so hard the knuckles were white, Virginia watched. Maybe Frank would go on. No, he was going to turn in! A sudden gust of rain obscured her vision, but when it cleared, she could see Father clinging to the side of the cart for dear life while Frank raced to the barn. Snatching up a shawl, Virginia sped outside.

"Oh, Father, are you all right?" she gasped.

"Yes, I'm all right." Father climbed down stiffly and unharnessed Frank. "I saw the storm coming up and thought you might need some help with the chicks, so I told Mike I'd come on ahead. He'll bring the team and wagon later."

"I got the chicks shut up and was just closing the windows when I heard Frank coming down the hill. I was afraid he'd throw you out when he turned into the lane."

"He just about did," Father conceded. "I decided to hang onto the cart and give him his head. I thought he'd surely stop when he came to the barn," Father laughed shakily.

"Well, it isn't funny! People are killed every day in accidents. It was terrible to see you coming so fast down the hill." Virginia felt the tears coming.

"God was with us, Virgie. I'm all right," Father said quietly, taking her arm. "And since you did such a good job here I can just set and think how lucky I am to have a grown-up girl."

Later Virginia told Mike about her scare. "I don't think you should let Father drive Frank in the road cart anymore, Mike. I don't think he can manage such a high-spirited horse."

"Well, I'll try to arrange it so it doesn't happen, Virginia, but you know I can't exactly tell Father he's not allowed to do something!" Mike replied.

On a Sunday early in June Elder Peters approached Father and Virginia at church. "Brother John, I wonder if you could help us out. You know we have some Dunker families living over near Rising. They've been talking about starting a church and are having some meetings next weekend. They want to have a council, but of course they need a minister to conduct it. We were wondering if you could go and help them."

"Well, Brother Peters, you know I only hold the second degree. Shouldn't this be an ordained man?"

"I suppose it really should, but you have good sound judgment and would be helping all of us out if you could do it, since neither Brother Hersler nor I can go. They want to have their council on Friday, I believe, so you'd need to go over then."

During the week it was planned that Father would go on the train on Friday. Virginia, Lottie and Lillie Burkholder, Lottie's cousin, would drive over on Saturday and return with Father on Monday. Lottie would drive their horse and buggy. Probably some others from their church would be going over for the weekend services also.

On Thursday, however, Lottie sent word that her mother had come down with summer complaint and she wouldn't be able to go. Virginia was disappointed. She'd been looking forward to this last adventure with Lottie before they were separated, and Lillie was a jolly girl, too. It would have been so much fun!

"Virginia, why don't you and Lillie take Fred and our buggy," suggested Mike. "Lottie was planning to stop at the Johnston's west of David City at noon. You could still do that. Fred's perfectly reliable and I'm sure you wouldn't have any trouble. Besides, a grown-up school teacher has to do lots of new things," he finished teasingly.

Virginia made a face at him. It still didn't seem possible that she might be teaching by fall! Maybe she could do this, after all, and it would be fun to go with Lillie, though she'd really miss Lottie.

They got started on Saturday in good time. It was a beautiful summer day, and for once was not too hot. Meadowlarks called from fence posts beside large fields of waving green corn. Proud pheasants broke from roadside cover and crossed in front of the buggy. Choke cherries grew in the ravines and along the fences.

"It makes my mouth twist just to look at a choke cherry tree," Lillie said. She was a tall girl, with dark hair, flashing black eyes and a merry laugh. "If times ever get better I'm going to buy oranges and apples every week!"

"Wouldn't that be wonderful?" agreed Virginia. "When I was a little girl in Kansas we saw oranges and apples only at Christmas. Now I see them more often but still can't buy them. Choke cherries aren't too bad, though, if you have enough sugar. The juice is pretty good when you eat them with cream."

"Sounds like a waste of good cream to me," Lillie said. "Maybe I should just eat the juice and throw the cherries out. Last year it was so dry that they were nothing but tough skin stretched over a seed. Do you know anyone at Rising?"

"I was born there and my mother is buried there," replied Virginia, "but—"

"Oh, yes, I remember," Lillie broke in.

"You remember? What do you mean?" Virginia questioned.

"Maybe I shouldn't have said anything about it," replied Lillie hesitantly. "But I remember being in church when the minister announced that Mrs. Wine, over at Rising, had died. So many people began crying that I wondered who in the world she was that everyone should be so upset. I was five then."

"Thank you for telling me that, Lillie," Virginia said thoughtfully. "I was only three when Mother died, and I know so little about her that I always want to hear whatever anyone can tell me. We left Rising to homestead in Kansas when I was five."

"Isn't this where we turn over to Johnstons?" Lillie interrupted, as they came to a crossroad.

"If we don't we'll end up in David City, and I'll be spending enough time there this summer without going today," irginia laughed, as she turned Fred to the right.

When they arrived at Johnston's the men took Fred to the stable and fed him. The Johnstons were really Lottie's friends and Virginia felt all her old shyness washing over her at first. But Lillie's merry chatter broke the ice and the Johnstons were friendly. Besides, Virginia thought—remembering Mike's statement—if I'm going to be a school teacher I'll have to go into lots of strange situations. Oh, dear, I think I'd rather just stay home and be a dumb goose!

Soon after dinner the girls started out again. They would need to keep going steadily to arrive in good time. After only an hour Fred began to sweat and slow down.

"I can't understand what's the matter with him," Virginia said. "It's gotten hotter, but not that hot. Pulling the buggy on this smooth hard road isn't nearly as hard as working in the fields, and that's what he does all week long. Why is he sweating so?"

Try as she might, Virginia couldn't hurry Fred. He walked slower and slower, plodding along as the hot, dry wind wilted the girls and curled the corn leaves.

"Well, we're only a couple of miles from Sutterman's where we're supposed to stay," Lillie said at last. "Oh, look at Fred!"

Fred was trying to lie down, still harnessed to the buggy and right in the road. Virginia flapped the reins on his broad roan back. "Come on, Fred, keep going. We can't stop here. We're almost there," she called encouragingly. Surely Father would be at Sutterman's and would know what was wrong.

At last Sutterman's farm came into view. Slowly, slowly, Fred plodded down the lane and into the farmyard. Mr.

124

Sutterman came out to meet them. "Well, we're glad to see you. We were beginning to wonder about you," he greeted them.

"I don't know why," Virginia replied, "but there's something wrong with the horse. Is my father here?"

"No, he's making visits with the deacons. We'll see him at church tonight. Say, you've got a mighty sick horse here," Mr. Sutterman said as he unhitched Fred, who sank to the ground. The girls struggled to help Mr. Sutterman get the harness off. Now they saw that Fred's stomach was distended and his eyes were glassy.

"I believe you girls had better go into the house," Mr. Sutterman said quietly. Virginia turned away, sick at heart. What a loss to the family if anything happened to Fred, such a good, steady work horse. If only Mike hadn't talked her into this venture. But then, she'd wanted to believe she could do it, so she shouldn't blame Mike.

"How—how is he?" she asked when Mr. Sutterman came in later.

"He's dead. We moved him out back."

In a daze Virginia cleaned up, ate supper and helped get ready for church. She tried to be friendly and answer when spoken to, but she hardly heard or saw what was going on. How could we have such bad luck in the middle of the summer when we need the horses in the fields so badly? What will Mike say?

They were almost late in arriving at the small schoolhouse where the meetings were held. It was very crowded and Virginia saw she wouldn't be able to get to Father right away. She and Lillie and the Sutterman girls squeezed into a bench near the back. She couldn't see the front, and it was very hot.

After the first hymn someone said, "Brother John Wine will lead us in prayer." At the sound of Father's familiar voice, coming through the strange crowd, the strain of the day overcame Virginia. She clenched her fists as the hot tears welled up.

"Kind and indulgent God, our Heavenly Father . . ."

125

She had heard that prayer so many times, beginning at Sunday School in the Lone Star schoolhouse back in Kansas. Father had been elected to the ministry as a young man, but had never been too active, serving more as a deacon than as a minister. Since they'd lived in Nebraska he'd done very little preaching, but often helped in the services and Virginia knew his prayer almost by heart. Yes, now he was remembering "the sick, the poor and the needy." He would pray for peace, too, asking that all might live so each could enjoy his "own vine and fig tree."

Virginia hoped no one was noticing as she wiped her eyes. Shedding a few tears had calmed her. She'd just have to wait through the service and tell Father the bad news as soon as she could.

After the service she waited until the congregation had moved out into the warm night. Her father came slowly down the aisle, talking to each person, it seemed to Virginia. Finally he reached her. "Hello, Pet, I see you made it all right."

"Oh, Father, I have such bad news! Something got the matter with Fred this afternoon and just after we got to Sutterman's, he—he died!"

"Oh, is that all?"

All? Virginia couldn't believe her ears. Surely she'd done something wrong, or Fred would still be alive. Hadn't Father heard what she said? Was he so involved in his church duties here that he'd forgotten how much they needed Fred at home? Well, at least she'd told him now, so it was no longer her worry alone.

On Monday morning they rode home with another family from Shrevesville, the buggy tied on behind. Virginia still couldn't believe that she wouldn't be blamed. Surely Mike would tell her what she'd done wrong. But Mike was no more worried than Father had been.

"I suppose the Johnston's gave him some fresh oats and starting out like that right away gave him fermentation. He was pretty old. I was going to sell him this fall anyway," Mike comforted her.

126

"Well, believe me, that's the last driving trip I make on my own! If we can't arrange to ride with someone back and forth to David City, I'll just forget Institute. I'm not going through that again," Virginia declared vigorously.

Chapter 19.
NEW VISTAS

Virginia was certainly glad Pearl was with her, that first week of Institute: new classes, teachers, classmates, a strange town, a landlady! She felt overwhelmed by all these new experiences at once. Pearl seemed so wise and at ease. Virginia shuddered to think of making so many adjustments by herself this fall when she began teaching. If only she and Pearl could teach together. But they would both be receiving Third Grade Certificates, so they could only teach one-room country schools, and of course they couldn't be together.

Virginia's quick mind found the new courses fairly easy, but she studied hard. There was so much to learn! It would be a disgrace not to pass the exams, especially since Pearl was paying her expenses. Besides, the thought of teaching frightened her. What if someone asked her a question she didn't know? It was one thing not to know all the answers in Sunday School, because no one knew all about God, but it would be quite another not to know the area of Russia, or how to parse a compound-complex sentence. She must study hard!

Even though they spent some time with other students from Shrevesville, Virginia was amazed to discover how much she missed the folks at home. She could hardly wait for Fridays to come. Those weekly rides back and forth were such fun! Usually someone from Shrevesville came after them, and there would be a spring wagon full of chat-

tering, laughing, singing young people. On Sunday night
the same group would return to David City.

On a Friday in the middle of August, David, Morris and
Lottie came for the Shrevesville group. On the way back
Morris drove the team, with two of the other boys beside
him, and David and Lottie joined the others in the back of
the wagon. There was much singing and laughter, but several times Virginia caught a look passing between David
and Lottie, a look she'd never noticed before.

Virginia didn't say anything to Pearl, but all the next
day as they washed and ironed, this new idea was growing.
Were Lottie and David becoming more than friends? Of
course they'd always been friendly, as everyone at church
was friendly. After all, they were her two best chums, so
that alone would make them friends, but there seemed to
be something more, or was her imagination running away
with her?

After church on Sunday, Virginia cornered Lottie. "Tell
me, did I see something between you and David on Friday
night, or did I just imagine it?"

"Why, I don't know what you mean, Virginia. I sat on
one side of the wagon and he sat on the other, so what could
have gotten between us? A grasshopper?" laughed Lottie.

"Lottie!" warned Virginia. "What's been going on behind
my back? What have you two been up to while I was studying my poor head off down in David City?"

"Oh, Virginia, nothing," Lottie said, but she was blushing. "He's just walked me home from Sunday-evening
church a few times. After all, you weren't here for either of
us to walk with!"

"And you like him—that way?"

"Oh, yes—oh, I don't know—oh, Virgie, please don't say
anything about it," stammered Lottie, blushing even more.

"Well, of course I won't Dear. Why shouldn't he walk
you home? After all, he was taking care of you fifteen years
ago, so why shouldn't he now?" Virginia laughed, referring
to a family story of eleven-year-old David being asked to
care for two-year-old Lottie while their mothers were busy

preparing a meal for church guests. "My favorite brother and my best friend! What could be better?" she exclaimed.

"Oh, Virgie, please don't say it like that!" Lottie pleaded. "David's so smart and I quit school so long ago. I feel like such a dunce sometimes."

"Why, Lottie Keller! You most certainly are not a dunce!" Virginia cried indignantly. "You're my best and dearest friend and nothing can change that. If this develops into something, no one will be happier than I, but even if it doesn't we'll go right on being best friends, won't we?"

"Of course we will, Virginia. Have a good week at school." Lottie called as she hurried after Mayme, "And good luck on your examinations."

Virginia watched her go, a whirlwind of feelings within her. Lottie and David? David and Lottie? How strange it seemed to say their names together. Here she'd been worrying about getting her Certificate and teaching school, and Lottie was experiencing a different part of growing-up. If this continued would it change anything between her and Lottie or her and David? Would that old feeling of being left out, that she'd had so much as a child, come back to plague her? Oh, dear, life was so complicated! But she couldn't worry about it now. This week was the end of school and Thursday would be Teachers' ffaminations.

Virginia and Pearl studied hard and tried not to think about Thursday, but finally it came. The examinations took all day and were harder than Virginia had expected.

"How did you do?" Pearl asked, when they were finally out of the stifling room.

"I don't know," Virginia answered wearily. "I think I passed, but right now I'm not sure of anything. Political geography wasn't as hard as I expected, but mathematics was much harder!"

"I thought so, too," Pearl agreed. "We'll just have to wait and see, but I know one thing. I'm certainly glad it's over."

All the next week they waited for the letter that would tell them if their summer's work had been in vain. Virginia thought she couldn't stand it if Pearl's long winter of working and saving would disappear with nothing to show for it.

On Friday when Pearl and Virginia walked to town, the letters were there! Standing in the dusty street, the girls opened the envelopes with trembling hands. Inside each, in fancy penmanship and huge, curling capitals, was a Third Grade Certificate, issued by the County Superintendent of Schools, Butler County, Nebraska.

From the Superintendent Pearl received a list of possible openings for beginning teachers. Most of the one-room schools would open in September, so they hadn't much time to contact the various schoolboards. Thus began a round of hot, dreary drives to see about schools. By the time the girls had dressed in their best clothes they were breathless from the heat, and when they had driven several miles through the late August dust, they felt too wilted to see anyone, much less someone who could give or withhold a teaching position.

After several interviews Pearl was awarded a country school, with a salary of twenty-five dollars per month. She would pay twelve of that for board and room in a home near the school.

Virginia made a few more contacts, but with no results. Most schools had already secured their teachers. Besides, "Our board feels you may be too young to handle some of our tougher boys," one board chairman explained.

So Virginia helped Pearl get her clothes and belongings ready, secretly a little relieved that she didn't have to teach. It felt strange to stay home when she knew school was starting in Shrevesville, but it had advantages, too. The whole round of housework was hers, and Virginia found that she liked handling it alone.

As she cut corn for drying on a late September day, Virginia thought how helpful Father was and always had been. Late last night he had gathered the sweet corn and put it in the cellar for the night. Early this morning he had the fire going under a big boiler of corn. Now she would cut it off and spread it on old sheets placed on the slope of the cellar doors. She would cover it with another old cloth to keep off flies, but she must still shoo the chickens away and bring it in every night or if a shower came up. When it was so dry it rattled, they could store it in a dry place until next winter. Virginia could almost taste its nutty flavor after it had been soaked and boiled, but now the sticky, milky juice spattered and stuck all over her clothes, the kitchen, the pans and utensils she was using. She could feel it drying on her face, and was grateful no one could see her.

They were in a hurry to get the early fall work done, because Nebraska District Meeting would be held at their church in October, and there was much to do in preparation. Everyone's home must be clean to receive as many guests as possible, and meals must be served to all who came. Father had been busy helping with arrangements. Entertaining the yearly gathering was a great experience in the church's life.

Chapter 20.
THE OPEN DOOR

"Oh, Virginia, isn't it exciting? I declare I'm so tired from helping Mother clean house for company that I don't know if I'm coming or going," Lottie groaned, as she reached for another potato.

Lottie, Virginia and Lillie Burkholder were peeling potatoes for the first meal of District Meeting. Swathed to their necks in big aprons, to protect their church dresses, they sat near the door of the food tent. Father and the committee had worked extremely hard in making preparations, and finally the great day had arrived. While the adults were concerned that all would go well, the young people were excited at the prospect of meeting old and new friends from other churches across Nebraska.

"My goodness, look how many are coming, and it's still early. I wonder if the men put up enough extra hitching racks," Virginia said.

"Well, that's easily fixed. It's the food I'm worried about. How are you coming with the potatoes, girls?" asked Sister Hersler as she came from the end of the tent, where two large cookstoves were covered with pots and pans. She peered out through the open tent flap. "Why, that's Mary Frantz and Hattie Netzly, so those wagons must be from Kearney. They're the ones who have started the Kearney mission, you know."

"A mission? What do you mean?" asked Virginia.

"Our Nebraska District is starting a mission in Kearney.

You know that's a wild town and there aren't many churches there. Last year at District Meeting we decided we should do something about it. Mary and Hattie have been there this summer and I guess have gotten it well started." Sister Hersler borrowed Virginia's knife to remove a scrap of peeling.

"Do we have a church there?" asked Lillie.

"We had a church out in the country, but I believe Brother Peters said they're going into town to worship now, to give more support to the mission. Well, I've got to get back to the stove. I believe another tub will be enough, girls." Sister Hersler filled a dishpan of peeled potatoes and left the girls alone.

"Gracious, Virginia, *who* is that young man?" breathed Lottie.

Virginia took a deep breath before she answered. She'd hardly heard Sister Hersler's conversation, she was trying so hard to calm her pounding heart and shaking hands.

"That—that's Ira Snavely, I think. He—he was at District Meeting last year," she murmured faintly.

"Is he from Kearney too?"

"I guess so, but I think he's been going to college. Last year he had been at Moody Bible Institute in Chicago."

"But isn't he *handsome*!" sighed Lillie, the potato forgotten in her hand.

The young man *was* handsome. He was short and well built, carrying himself with confidence. The autumn sun brought out auburn glints in his dark hair and beard. His jaw jutted out as he talked with Brother Peters.

"He's wearing a Brethren coat. Is he a minister?" asked Lottie.

"Last year they said he was Nebraska's youngest preacher," explained Virginia. She was beginning to get control of herself. There was no reason for her to feel so giddy. After all, she hadn't even thought of him for a year, and he certainly wouldn't remember her from last District Meeting. He was educated and experienced, and she was just a little girl who couldn't even get a school to teach. But she wished her fingers weren't all wrinkled from the dirty potato water. She must be sure to clean her nails when she finished the potatoes.

During the evening service a report was given on the Kearney mission. It was well started, but Mary Frantz was leaving and a helper must be found for Hattie Netzly. In fact, the District leaders wanted to find a helper during this meeting.

After the service, Virginia, Lottie and David joined the large group of young people outside the meeting tent. Everyone wanted to be friendly, but there were some strained silences, as they didn't yet feel acquainted. With his usual poise, David stepped into this situation.

"Well, now, since we're going to be together all weekend, I think we'd better get acquainted. I'm David Wine. I'll introduce the ones from here and the rest of you will have to tell us your names. This is Morris Keller, his sisters Lottie and Mayme, Lillie Burkholder, my sister Virginia . . ."

"Virginia! That's the name! I knew I remembered those blue eyes from last year!" broke in a hearty voice. "I'm Ira Snavely, and this is . . ." His voice was lost in hearty laughter at Virginia's expense. In the darkness she felt her cheeks burning. He remembered! After a whole year at college with all those girls, he remembered her! Now, don't be a goose, she told herself. He only said he remembered your eyes!

The next day there were appeals for a helper at the mission. After the evening service Brother Peters approached Virginia. "Wirchie, have you thought about going to Kearney with Sister Hattie? You didn't get a school to teach, and now you could answer this call," he stated convincingly.

"Oh—I—I don't think so," murmured Virginia in embarrassment. "I'm much too young."

After she had seen to their guests' comfort that night, Virginia tossed and turned in her half of the bed. Pearl had come home from her school to attend the rest of District Meeting and was sleeping with Virginia, so there would be more room for guests. I guess I'm restless because I'm not used to sleeping with someone, Virginia thought. She kept remembering Brother Peters' astonishing question, but of course it was unthinkable. Who would take care of Father if she went to Kearney?

Ira Snavely hadn't paid any attention to Virginia after his first remark about her eyes. At least, she didn't think so. A couple of times she thought she'd caught him looking at her, but she couldn't be sure. He'd given a strong talk in support of the mission that day, ending with a request for more workers. Virginia had learned that he helped with the preaching there whenever he was home from McPherson College. He was going to preach at the Saturday morning service. He had proved to be a livewire in every session and even the older folks were looking forward to his sermon.

The next morning the church was full and the message alive, not like so many sermons they heard. Brother Ira used a consecration subject, "The Everlasting Service" and the text was Exodus 21:2-6. Virginia listened, fascinated, as Ira compared the rules for Hebrew servants to the idea of lifelong service to God. What would it be like to go to college, to learn so much, and to get so many new ideas? It made her head ache to think of it, but what a challenge it would be!

During the noon hour, more of the local people suggested to Virginia that she should go to Kearney. When the afternoon service was finished, Hattie Netzley herself approached.

"Virginia," she said pleasantly, "so many people from your local church here are saying you would be good help at the mission. I'd like to get acquainted."

"Oh, Sister Netzly," Virginia replied hesitantly. "I don't know why they keep saying that. Surely there must be someone older and more experienced. I—I just graduated from high school!"

"Well, you know, that's more education than a lot of our people have. Let me tell you about our work and maybe you'll decide you could help, after all. Mary and I have been trying to help the mothers in the poorer section of Kearney. We've begun sewing classes, reading circles and meetings to discuss their problems and try to get across some ideas of cleanliness and health. Of course, we have prayer meetings, Bible study and home visitation, too. Since Mary's leaving we really need someone to help with the music and I believe you've had some training in that, haven't you?"

"Yes, I—I have learned quite a lot at our Musical Union rehearsals and concerts. I didn't think of doing all those things at the mission."

"Well, we're trying to meet as many needs of the people as we can. I'm sure you'd find many ways to help. Won't you think about it? We would give you your board and two dollars a week."

"Yes, I—I'll think about it. But I don't think I should leave my father."

When the house was quiet that night, Virginia came out to the kitchen, thinking she might make some preparations for morning. Father was sitting on the daybed, where he would sleep.

"Father, I—I guess you know what people have been saying to me," Virginia said as she set the table as quietly as possible.

"Yes, Pet, they've been talking to me, too," replied Father.

"I keep remembering what you said last spring when Pearl offered to pay my way to Teachers' Institute. You said, When doors open for us we should walk through them, even if we don't know where they will take us.' I thought that was a big enough door, and now here's another one."

"Yes, that's the way life is. We never know what lies ahead," Father replied.

"But I don't understand. I went through that door, but I didn't get a school." Virginia pleated the dish towel nervously.

"Perhaps God had this in mind for you all the time, Vir-

137

gie, but you needed the experience of going away this summer. Don't you think God will give you strength and guidance at the mission?"

"Oh, of course He will, but I thought He wanted me to stay with you. After all, you need help, too."

"It's been a wonderful thing to have you here this fall, Virginia, but you mustn't give up your life for Mike and me. We'll get along, if you think you'd like to help. It's not so far. Maybe we could call you home if we got in a terrible scrape!" Father started to laugh, but stopped abruptly.

With eyes full of tears, Virginia went into his arms. He held her tightly, his beard tickling her face. "My little Virgie," he whispered. "My little Virgie that's a grown-up lady now. How I wish your mother could see you!"

"Maybe she does, Father," whispered Virginia. "Maybe she does."

The next day, Virginia met with Hattie Netzley and the Mission Board and told them she'd go to Kearney *until they found* someone. Everyone heard of it, and many people offered their best wishes. Ira Snavely's mother welcomed Virginia warmly to Kearney.

"You must come out to the farm to visit us. Ira'll be going back to McPherson, but the youngest two are still at home and the girls get home from teaching sometimes," she urged.

"Thank you, I'd like to come, but I'm sure I'll be pretty busy at the mission," replied Virginia shyly.

District Meeting closed with an inspiring service on Sunday night. The next morning, the visitors took their leave of the families where they'd been staying, and the local congregation was left with much straightening up to do.

Virginia was especially busy. She'd promised to go to Kearney in early November. There were things around the house she wanted to finish for Father before she left and she had her own things to get ready.

One day Mike came home from town with several packages. "Virginia, here are some things I thought you might need."

"Why, Mike, you shouldn't spend your money on me," protested Virginia, as she peeked in the bags. A lovely warm shawl was in one of them and in another a clothes brush.

"Well, I don't buy things for young ladies very often, so let me do it when I have a chance," laughed Mike. I was wondering, too, if you'd like to have my trunk. I'm not using it and it might be handy to put your things in."

"Oh, that would be wonderful, Mike. I certainly could use it. You've always been such a good brother to me."

"Well, now, don't get sentimental on me, or I might take it back," teased Mike.

At last the day for the final packing arrived. As she worked in her room, Virginia looked at herself appraisingly in the mirror. Sometimes she'd wondered how it would look to soften her brown hair a little above her forehead, but of course now that she was going to be a mission worker she must keep it simple and plain.

How strange it seemed to be packing to leave home. But she really wouldn't be so far away, and she was only going until they found someone else. Last spring she never would have believed it if someone had told her she'd be a mission worker in Kearney by fall. I guess it's a good thing we can't see into the future, Virginia thought.

Near the top of the trunk she placed her best things, some dainty handkerchiefs from Lottie and a pair of good wool gloves from David. She didn't even want to think how much she would miss both of them, but they and others had promised to visit the mission. And, somehow, leaving them in each other's care made it easier. She was not really upset at the idea of Lottie and David together. Nothing could change the wonderful relationship she had with each of them, and if their friendship should develop into marriage, that would just tie them more closely to her.

Strangely, every time she thought of Lottie and David together, she thought of Ira. That was silly, because she really didn't have anything to base it on. He'd never said anything, or singled her out, after his remark that first

139

night. And, of course, by this time he'd returned to Mc-Pherson College.

And yet—and yet, there was the autograph album. Virginia's face burned with shame as she wondered how bold Ira must think she was. She had taken the album to church on the last night of District Meeting so some of her new girl friends could write in it. Other albums were being passed around and Virginia had lost track of hers for a little while as she wrote. The next day she was amazed to discover that Ira had made an entry.

Virginia blushed now as the book fell open to that page. It was just a Bible verse, of course. What would be more appropriate for a preacher to write? And yet—did it have another meaning? Surely not, but her heart beat faster as she read it again, breathlessly.

"Sister Virginia,
"The Lord watch between me and thee, when we are absent one from another. Gen. 31:49
Yours in Jesus,
I.C.S."